J. T. EDSON'S
FLOATING OUTFIT

The toughest bunch of Rebels that ever lost a war, they fought for the South, and then for Texas, as the legendary Floating Outfit of "Ole Devil" Hardin's OD Connected ranch.

MARK COUNTER was the best-dressed man in the West; always dressed fit-to-kill. BELLE BOYD was as deadly as she was beautiful, with a "Manhattan" model Colt tucked under her long skirts. THE YSABEL KID was Comanche fast and Texas tough. And the most famous of them all was DUSTY FOG, the ex-cavalryman known as the Rio Hondo Gun Wizard.

J. T. Edson has captured all the excitement and adventure of the raw frontier in this magnificent Western series. Turn the page for a complete list of Berkley Floating Outfit titles.

J. T. EDSON'S
FLOATING OUTFIT
WESTERN ADVENTURES
FROM BERKLEY

J.T. Edson

THE TOWN TAMERS

BERKLEY BOOKS, NEW YORK

This Berkley book contains the complete
text of the original edition.
It has been completely reset in a typeface
designed for easy reading, and was printed
from new film.

THE TOWN TAMERS

A Berkley Book/published by arrangement with
Transworld Publishers Ltd.

PRINTING HISTORY
Corgi edition published 1969
Berkley edition/May 1985

ISBN: 0-425-07682-2

A BERKLEY BOOK® TM 757,375
Berkley Books are published by The Berkley Publishing Group,
200 Madison Avenue, New York, New York 10016.
The name "BERKLEY" and the stylized "B"
with design are trademarks belonging to
Berkley Publishing Corporation.
PRINTED IN THE UNITED STATES OF AMERICA

For "Mum" Thompson, to help her
convince people I really am her
son-in-law.

AUTHOR'S NOTE. These stories originally appeared as a strip-cartoon in *The Victor* and I extend my gratitude to Messrs. D. C. Thomson & Co. Ltd., for allowing me to turn them into a book.

PART ONE

Governor Mansfield's Prerogative

"They're coming, Mr. Galt!"

After running the length of Trail End's main street the excited youngster could no more than gasp out his news on arrival. For all that his words carried to more ears than those attached to the fat, pompous skull of Mayor Joseph Galt. Even those of the people lining the main street who could not hear the message received it from other citizens closer to the speaker. Hushed expectancy settled on the assembled population as they waited to witness what promised to be a momentous occasion.

For the first time in living memory the Governor of Kansas had exercised his prerogative by appointing the entire marshal's office staff into one of his State's towns. Normally the election of civic law enforcement officers rested in the citizens' hands; which had brought about the conditions that called for the Governor's intervention.

Born as a shipping point for the great herds of cattle brought north from Texas to the railroad, Trail End competed with other such towns in Kansas and was, by repute, the most evil of them all. Its current marshal, a hulking, dullwitted brute named Jackley, lacked every quality needed to make even a moderately good peace officer. While capable of working over a very drunk cowhand or other visitor, he made no attempt to check the blatant exploitation and dishonesty practiced by many of the citizens.

It had been Jackley's sole talent which brought about Governor Mansfield's intervention. After taking a brutal beating from the marshal while in jail, a young Texas cowhand had died. True, an obliging coroner affirmed that a heart-seizure caused the inconsiderate cowhand's death. So the matter ought to have ended there.

Unfortunately the deceased cowhand possessed a number of loyal kin-folk, the most prominent being one, Shanghai Pierce, respected rancher and very influential in the affairs of the Lone Star State, a man whose many friends included several of Texas' top-grade fighting sons. Word had it that the dead cowhand had been the rancher's favorite nephew, come north as a trail hand to gather practical experience in the family's business.

General Mansfield foresaw grave repercussions as a result of the murder—for the cowhand's death amounted to nothing less than that. Unlike the more liberal—and therefore more bigoted—members of the State Legislature, Mansfield recognized just how much the prosperity of Kansas depended on the Texas trail herds. Unless steps were taken, and taken rapidly, that vital source of wealth might be lost. Even if the Texans could not find another way of shipping their cattle to the East, tensions between them and the Kansans were sure to be at boiling point. One incident, sparked off by either side, might see the Sunflower State involved in the bloodiest strife since the end of the Civil War.

With that in mind, Mansfield looked over his crop of lawmen and found none who might satisfy Shanghai Pierce that he truly intended to purge the plague spot. No Texan would trust the Earp brothers. Bat Masterson held down Dodge City too well to be removed. Nor could Wild Bill Hickok be pulled out of Abilene, even if his reputation among the trail crews had made him acceptable.

Then Mansfield remembered a name, a man to fit his needs. Probably the only person Shanghai Pierce would regard as proof of the Governor's good intentions. The man Mansfield selected to clean up Trail End ranked high on the Texans' roll of honor. During the war, as a cavalry captain only seventeen years old, he built a fame equaled only by Dixie's other pair of master military raiders, Turner Ashby and John Singleton Mosby. When peace came, he took over as segundo on the great OD Connected ranch, only to be sent on a dangerous and delicate mission into trouble-torn Mexico. By bringing it off successfully, he helped avert a clash between the two countries.* Since then he had carved his name as master cowhand, trail boss second to none. More than that, he possessed experience as a peace officer gained wearing a badge in two tough wild towns.† Texans boasted of his uncanny bare-hand fighting skill and told many tales about his amazing dexterity in the use of a fast-drawn brace of Colt Peacemakers. Many called him the Rio Hondo gun wizard—his name was Dusty Fog.

If any man could satisfy Shanghai Pierce of the Governor's good intentions and earnest desire to right the wrong, Dusty Fog was he.

No one man, not even the fabled Rio Hondo gun wizard, could tame a town like Trail End alone. He would need trusted deputies, tough, loyal, efficient backing and support. In that respect Dusty Fog could claim to be ideally supplied.

To help work their outer ranges, the great ranches of Texas operated floating outfits. Four to six men, depending on the work involved, traveled the distant areas accom-

*Told in *The Ysabel Kid*.

†Told in *The Trouble Busters, The Making of a Lawman* and *Quiet Town*.

panied by a chuckwagon, or took food on mule-back, and acted as a mobile ranch crew. The OD Connected's floating outfit supplied Dusty Fog with exactly the kind of men he needed to tame Trail End.

Take Mark Counter, Dusty's right bower and able second in command. Six foot three in height, an exceptionally handsome Hercules of a man, something of a dandy in dress yet a top-hand with cattle. While his enormous strength and skill in a rough-house brawl received much acclaim, his ability in the gun-fighting line gained less due to riding in the shadow of the fastest man of all. Yet practical critics with great personal experience in such matters credited him with being second only to Dusty Fog in the matter of rapidity of draw and accurate shooting. Such a man would be invaluable to Dusty in the days ahead.

Nor would the Ysabel Kid, third in the hierarchy of the floating outfit, prove less useful. Born the only child of a wild Irish Kentuckian father and a French Creole *Pehnane* Comanche mother, the Kid grew up among the latter's people. From his grandfather, Long Walker the *Pehnane* war chief, he learned those things every brave-heart warrior needed at his command to make a success among the toughest of the horse-Indian tribes.* Silent movement, locating hidden enemies and avoiding being seen at the wrong moment, skill at reading sign, ability with weapons and superb horsemanship came almost as second nature to the Kid, taught well and eager to acquire the knowledge. Less of a gunfighter—in the accepted Western sense—than his companions, he claimed few peers at handling a knife and less in the accurate use of a Winchester rifle.

No honest lawman would have despised having the remaining two members of the floating outfit at his side. Though young, Waco—he owned no other name—knew law enforcement work real well. Left an orphan almost from birth by an Indian attack, he had been raised by a North

*Told in *Comanche*.

Texas rancher. At fourteen he rode the ranges and spent every cent that could be spared on ammunition for a worn old Navy Colt, gravitating to Clay Allison's wild-onion CA crew. When Dusty Fog saved the youngster from death beneath the hooves of the stampeding CA herd,* Waco already possessed considerable skill in drawing and shooting. Joining the OD Connected, Waco learned when to use his guns and gave the Rio Hondo gun wizard the respect that might have gone to the father he never knew. Tough, capable, shrewd, his youthful exuberance controlled by the teaching of the other members of the floating outfit, Waco was likely to prove an asset in the marshal's office.

Formally a member of the Wedge, an outfit of trail drivers who ran herds north for ranchers unable to make the journey themselves, Doc Leroy possessed many talents which Dusty Fog could utilize in the fight to tame Trail End. Christened Marvin Eldridge Leroy, his nickname rose from a knowledge of medical work. Although Doc never graduated from the Eastern medical school, due to family troubles, he learned all he could and probably possessed more knowledge of treating gunshot wounds than any noted surgeon in the East. Nor did his skill end at removing bullets. When needed he could plant them home with speed and accuracy. In addition he knew much about the ways dishonest players improved their chances at gambling games and would place that specialized knowledge at Dusty's disposal.

All in all, given such able backing, Dusty Fog stood a better than fair chance of carrying out Governor Mansfield's wishes; a prospect which Mayor Galt did not view with the favor one might expect of such an important civic official.

"Give the boy a nickel, Elwin," the mayor said, for he never parted with money himself unless forced by dire necessity.

The tall, gangling, mournful-faced local undertaker dipped a hand into his pocket. Producing a coin with an expression

*Told in *Trigger Fast*.

of distaste, Elwin passed it to the boy. Then, waiting until the youngster withdrew from ear-shot, he turned to Galt.

"You'll have to make it plain that we don't want them running the law here, Joe. Folks'll expect it."

"After Mansfield sent them?" the mayor snorted. "You saw his letter. It's them or a *full* investigation into the running of the town. Backed by the State Militia if necessary."

Which point, the undertaker fully appreciated, meant trouble if not jail for both himself and Galt.

"There'll be plenty don't like it," Elwin commented.

"Jackley's one of 'em," Galt answered. "When I told him, he swore that no damned beef-head fast-gun's going to shove him out of office."

Turning his head, Mayor Galt looked along the wheel-rutted, hoof-scarred street to where five riders were approaching in a loose V-shaped formation. With considerable interest he studied the quintet and tried to decide their identity.

The tall, wide shouldered, handsome blond-haired youngster at the far left must be Waco. Tight-rolled and knotted about his throat, a bandana trailed long ends over his grey shirt and black and white calf-skin vest. His brown Levis pants hung cowhand style outside his boots, the cuffs turned back to act as a receptacle for nails or other small items when performing work requiring them. Around his lean waist hung a gunbelt, matched staghorn-handled Colt Artillery Peacemakers in the contoured fast-draw holsters. Young he might be, but those guns were no mere decoration. He rode a huge paint stallion, sitting its low-horned, double-girthed Texas saddle with easy grace. Following without fuss or fighting the rope from it to the paint's saddle, a pack-horse carried the floating outfit's bedrolls and war-bags.

To the youngster's right hand, showing just as much ease at straddling a large black horse, sat Doc Leroy. An inch shorter than Waco, he lacked the youngster's shoulder width. Though pallid, his studious face showed strength, his lack of color stemming from possessing a tan-resisting skin. Dressed cowhand style, he wore a short jacket with the right side stitched back to leave uninterrupted access to the ivory butt of the Colt Civilian Model Peacemaker hanging low on his leg.

One did not need the powers of an Indian medicine man to guess the name of the rider on the right flank. Dressed in all black range clothes, only the walnut handle of the old Dragoon Colt butt-forward in the low cavalry-draw holster at high right thigh and the ivory hilt of the James Black bowie knife sheathed on the left of his belt relieved the somber hue. His Indian-dark, almost babyish handsome features carried an expression of innocence only dispelled by his wild red-hazel eyes. After seeing them, nobody continued to regard the Ysabel Kid as young or innocent. Six foot tall, lean as a grease-wood fed steer, tough as whang-leather, he sat his huge, magnificent white stallion with the loose-limbed ease of a *Pehnane* Comanche. From under his left leg showed the butt of the "One of a Thousand" Winchester Model 1873 rifle he had won against some exceedingly talented opposition at the Cochise County Fair.*

Next to the Kid rode a man who might easily be Dusty Fog. Six foot three in height, golden blond, curly hair topping an almost classically handsome face, great spreading shoulders, arms which hinted at their enormous muscular development, a slender waist and long, powerful legs. That was the appearance one might expect of the legendary Rio Hondo gun wizard. A costly white Stetson with a silver-concha-decorated band started an expensive, made-to-measure somewhat dandyish cowhand's apparel. White ivory butted, and of the finest Best Citizen's Finish, the long

*Told in *Gun Wizard*.

barreled Colt Cavalry Peacemakers were fighting weapons and rode in a gun-rig tooled for extreme speed. He sat his enormous bloodbay stallion with grace, a light rider despite his giant size.

Yet if the blond giant should be Dusty Fog, Galt could not decide where Mark Counter might be, nor figure out the identity of the small, insignificant man in the center of the party.

True, the fifth man rode a paint stallion as large and well-developed as the other four horses, but he faded into nothing compared with his companions. Not more than five foot six in height, he looked like a nobody and not even the two bone-handled Colt Civilian Model Peacemakers riding butt-forward in the cross-draw holsters of an exceptionally well-designed and made gunbelt seemed to increase his stature or notice-ability. A good-looking young man, although not in the eye-catching way of the others, from hat to boots he spelled Texas cowhand. Just how he came to be in the quintet, Galt could not imagine. The mayor's mind ignored the obvious possibility. It seemed impossible that such a diminutive figure could belong to the man called Dusty Fog.

Two prominent saloon owners watched the Texans' arrival with scowling faces. Being recently arrived from the East, one of them let out a contemptuous snort.

"They don't look to amount to all the fuss there's been made," he said.

"That's what I thought the first time I saw them," his more experienced competitor answered. "Trouble was I didn't stay thinking it for long. You mark my words, Eggars, this town's done as long as they're here."

"Maybe they won't stop."

"I'd not hold my breath until they go, was I you. Say, I don't reckon you'd want to buy my place, would you?"

Clucks of disapproval rose from various of the town's "good" ladies as they gathered to view the new arrivals. To them Texan meant a wild, drunken cowhand on the spree. None of them remembered that the same men supplied them with their major source of income. As one sharp-featured female pillar of the local church put it:

"I can't see why Governor Mansfield had to ask Texans, and such young ones, into our town."

"That nice Mr. Earp and his brothers would have been much more satisfactory, I'm sure," another of the group went on; a view Mayor Galt and various worried businessmen might have heartily seconded.

From their vantage point on the balcony of Eggars' Educated Thirst Saloon, several not so good ladies also studied the Texans, although from a different aspect and point of view.

"Just look at that hunk of man!" sighed one, eyeing the blond giant with an ecstatic sigh. "I'd go with him for free—and like it."

"You should be so lucky," a second girl answered. "One thing's for sure. Happen the boss don't change his ways, we'll be looking for another town. That Cap'n Fog don't play around, I remember him in Quiet Town. He moves fast and real permanent."

Not all the audience felt doubts about the newcomers. The railroad depot's yard-master spat laconically into the dust and turned to his neighbor.

"Now maybe this stinking town'll get a clean-out," he said.

"Not happen some folks get their wantings, Dinger," the other, owner of a small general store, replied dismally.

Apparently ignoring the people on the sidewalks, the five Texans continued riding in the direction of the building which housed the marshal's office and jail. Curiosity, annoyance, open resentment or plain indifference showed on many of the faces, but just a few appeared hopeful that the future might be an improvement on the past.

"We done got us a welcome committee," drawled the Ysabel Kid, nodding to the fat, pompous and well-dressed shape of the mayor and the lean, lugubrious, but obviously prosperous Elwin who stood clear of the other folks before the office. "Which same I don't reckon the welcome'll be any too warm."

"They sure haven't turned the band out for us," replied the blond giant.

"Ain't started shooting at us yet, neither," Waco put in cheerfully. "Which same's something."

"You just haven't given them time to start, boy," Doc Leroy informed him.

Then they lapsed into silence. Four of the men brought their horses to a halt while the fifth advanced and stopped before Mayor Galt. Reaching up his left hand, he tilted back his black Stetson on his curly dusty blond hair.

"You'll be Mayor Galt, I reckon," the smallest of the quintet said, studying the sweat-dappled, fat, moustached face. "Likely the Governor told you about me. The name's Dusty Fog."

For a moment Galt stood speechless and immobile, trying to take in what he had just heard. Then slowly, as he stared at the small Texan, certain facts began to sink into his head. While the clothing might look like somebody's cast-offs, they had cost as much and had been as well-tailored as those worn by the blond giant. That small frame packed a surprising muscular development. If they had been the same height, Dusty Fog would have been at least as well-built as Mark Counter. A closer inspection showed Dusty's face to have strength of will, intelligence and he exuded a power of command no amount of mere size could give. Small he might be, but Dusty Fog stood in no man's shadow.

With an effort Galt regained control of himself. Putting on his best "win-friends-influence-people-and-grab-the-votes" smile, he nodded graciously.

"Good afternoon, Captain Fog," he greeted.

"Mind if we get the formalities over, Mayor?" Dusty asked. "I want to make a start at the chore."

"There's a slight snag to my swearing you in, Captain," Galt boomed back.

"You mean you don't aim to do it?" Dusty said mildly.

"I can hardly overrule the Governor's prerogative—even if I wanted to," Galt hastened to answer. "It's your predecessor—"

"What about him?"

"He's in the office and states that he won't hand over to you."

"Does, huh?"

"He most certainly does. Why don't you and your men go in and evict him?"

"Just him?" Dusty said with a dry smile.

"Town never needed even one deputy afore," Elwin put in.

Tossing his leg across the saddle, Dusty dropped to the ground. He flipped the paint's reins over the hitching rail and clearly considered that to be all the securing it needed.

"If he's on his own I shouldn't need any help," Dusty commented, knowing that he must handle the matter alone if he hoped to control the town.

Although the other four dismounted and ranged their horses alongside the big paint, none of them offered to follow Dusty into the office. Mark Counter and Doc Leroy remained on the street, but the other two stepped up to the sidewalk. Going to where they could look into the office, in case Galt was lying as to the number of men inside, Waco and the Ysabel Kid leaned on the wall at either side of the window.

"Fog's got to go in alone," Galt whispered to Elwin, watching Dusty enter the office. "If he doesn't, he might as well quit now."

"You paying to bury Jackley?" the undertaker inquired.

"He's not stupid enough to try gun-play against Dusty Fog," Galt replied. "And, unless Fog guns him down—shoots an *unarmed* man—Jackley'll tear him limb from limb."

At which point the conspirators heard Waco speak and what the youngster said told them that their plan to defeat or discredit the Governor's appointee had made its start.

"That big feller's going to hit Dusty," the youngster announced in a concerned voice.

"I can't hardly bear to watch," replied the Kid with a remarkable tranquility, considering what he could see.

Stepping into the office, Dusty looked around him with distaste. In general layout it differed from many other such places in only minor details. On the wall stood a rack of Winchester rifles and twin-barreled shotguns supplied by the town in case of emergency. Dusty noted all of them needed attention. Another early requisite would be the cleaning of the desk placed in the center of the room and a good sweeping of the floor would be further priority. To one side the safe stood open, key in its door and shelves empty. Beyond the desk a door opened on the line of cells. Their keys dangled on a ring which hung by the door along with a wicked-looking club.

Seated at the desk, Marshal Jackley studied the new arrival through bleary, bloodshot eyes. A big, burly, crop-haired man with a whiskery, sullen face, he wore a dirty shirt, town pants, supported by suspenders, and heavy boots. On rising, he allowed Dusty to see that he did not have a gun on his person.

"What might you want?" Jackley demanded.

"Your badge," Dusty replied. "I'm taking over here."

Never a quick thinker, it took Jackley a few seconds to absorb the meaning of the words. Then he let out a sharp snort and stamped around the desk. On first seeing Dusty enter, the marshal had taken him for a young cowhand calling on business. To learn the Governor of Kansas planned his replacement by that short-growed, no-account runt sent Jackley's hang-over inspired temper boiling over. The previous night Eggars and various other interested citizens had treated their marshal in a most liberal manner to drinks. Knowing his temper on the morning after a session of battling with John Barleycorn and wrestling the Old Stump-

Blaster, they figured Jackley ought to be primed to defend his position of honor against the new marshal. Clearly the men involved possessed a shrewd judgment of character.

Fuming with rage, Jackley rushed at the small, apparently unprepared Texan. Everything appeared to be in the marshal's favor: height, weight, ability, for natives of the Lone Star State tended to restrict their fighting to the use of guns. Unfortunately Jackley failed to realize he faced one Texan who knew plenty about bare-handed defense. Down in the Rio Hondo a small Oriental thought to be Chinese worked as servant to Dusty's uncle, Ole Devil Hardin. In reality Tommy Okasi hailed from Japan. Nobody knew why he had left his homeland, but he brought with him a very thorough knowledge of certain Oriental arts. To Dusty, smallest of the Hardin, Fog and Blaze boys, Tommy Okasi passed on the secrets of *ju-jitsu* and *karate*, placing in his hands a wonderfully efficient method of dealing with larger, heavier men.

As Jackley bore down on him, reaching out with powerful hands, Dusty moved. Catching the man's right forearm in his left hand, he bent to shoot his right arm between the man's legs and caught hold of the pants just behind the right knee. Before Jackley realized things were not going as planned, Dusty carried the trapped arm upwards and drew the man across his own shoulders. Using his attacker's momentum to augment his own surprising strength, Dusty pivoted and hurled Jackley away. Too late he saw the direction in which he had aimed the marshal. With a howl of mingled amazement and rage, Jackley crashed through the window.

"Now that's a neat departure from office," drawled the Kid as Jackley appeared in a cloud of flying glass.

"It sure hasn't done the window any good," Waco replied.

Landing with a crash on the sidewalk, Jackley bounced across it to light down on the street almost at the other two

Texans' feet. Slowly he forced himself into a sitting position, glaring around dazedly and then started to rise, muttering a variety of curses.

"Was I you, I'd give it up," Mark told him benevolently. "Wouldn't you, Doc?"

"I sure would, Mark," Doc answered. "That kind of thing's plumb hard on the veins."

Sage advice, handed out with the best intentions in the world; but Jackley clearly did not intend to profit by it. Coming to his feet, he glared around him. An almost bestial rage twisted his face as he charged towards the building from which he had been so unceremoniously evicted. Silence fell on the crowd, after a brief outburst of surprised chatter greeting Jackley's appearance. Every eye went to the six-foot tall, one-hundred-and-eighty-pound frame of the marshal comparing it with the small, insignificant man who had entered the office to evict him. Various emotions filled the audience, ranging from hope and jubilation to pity and despair.

"I'll kill him!" promised Jackley in a roar like that of a winter-starved grizzly bear. "I'll tear him apart."

The Ysabel Kid watched the hulking brute thunder into the office and shook his head sadly. "Now there goes a man who ain't showing what I'd call real good sense," he commented.

When Jackley burst in, Dusty was ready for him. Clearly the trip through the window, assisted by a *kata-guruma* shoulder-wheel throw had not dampened the marshal's rage or made him willing to turn over his badge of office. That suited Dusty, for young Pierce Audley, the dead cowhand, had been his friend.

As always Jackley relied purely on weight and muscle, a dangerous procedure when tangling with a man well-versed in the gentle arts of *ju-jitsu* and *karate*. Meeting the man's rush, Dusty sent him flying across the office with no greater difficulty than when tossing him through the window. When Jackley rose and attacked again, the small Texan went under his reaching arms. Holding his hand in the way taught to him as most suitable for the occasion, Dusty thrust his extended fingers savagely into the pit of Jackley's belly. While the *hiranukite,* the level-piercing hand blow of *karate,* might look strange and awkward to Occidental eyes, Jackley might have testified to its efficiency. Halted in his tracks, feeling as if his belly had rammed into a wooden post, the marshal croaked in agony and started to double over.

With his man so ideally placed, Dusty showed that he could also fight in the fashion of the western world. Up whipped his other hand, knotted into a fist that collided against Jackley's offered jaw. The marshal lifted erect again, to take a driving left cross against the side of his already throbbing chin. Spun around by the force of the blow, he crashed into the wall by the door to the cells. Close to his hand hung a means to counter the deadly techniques of that *big* Texan.

Spitting blood, Jackley closed his fingers around the club and jerked his leather thong free of the peg. With that deadly weapon in his hand he turned and slashed a savage blow at the advancing Texan. Just in time Dusty jerked his body backwards and the club hissed by him. Catching his balance, Jackley swung his weapon up and launched it downwards in an attempt to strike Dusty's head. Again he missed, but brought the club across and upwards in a backhand swing. Twisting away from the man, Dusty dropped forward on to his hands. As the club whistled above him he delivered a snap kick straight into the marshal's groin. Caught there by the heel of a cowhand boot, designed to spike into the ground and hold firm when roping on foot, Jackley gave a screech of pain and collapsed, the club clattering from his limp fingers.

Dusty rose, swung around, and his boot drove up again. It caught Jackley full under the jaw as he went down. For a moment Dusty thought he had kicked too hard. Jackley's head snapped back until his nose seemed to point at the roof, while his downward progress halted. Pitching to one side, the marshal measured his full length on the floor and lay still. Advancing, Dusty bent over to unpin the tarnished badge from Jackley's shirt and make sure that the other would recover, eventually, from the kick. Then the small Texan walked across the room towards the front door.

Silence dropped on the office after the shouts, crashes and other sounds which had followed Jackley's return. Mayor Galt and Elwin exchanged glances, hope showing on their faces.

"Maybe Jackley's finished him off," Elwin said hopefully.

"If he has, Fog's pards'll kill him," Galt answered. "Which won't be a bad thing. Jackley'd be nothing but trouble for us and we can use his death as an ex—"

At which point the mayor's dreams of an easy and satisfactory solution to the town's problems ended abruptly, crashing in ruins as Dusty Fog strolled calmly into view. Unmarked, not even breathing hard, the small Texan stood pinning the town marshal's badge on to his vest.

All too well Dusty knew the value of carefully performed dramatics as an aid to a peace officer's work. While he cared little one way or the other on a personal basis, he realized that his acceptance as town marshal would be made easier by his present display. Only by an effort did he hold down a grin at the sight of Galt's and Elwin's shocked, amazed expressions.

"Lon, Waco," Dusty said. "Get him hauled out of there. If he needs doctoring, see to it. Then as soon as he can ride tell him to get the hell out of Trail End and *pronto*."

In Spanish "pronto" meant fast, but when a Texan used it, the connotation went further. Then "*pronto*" implied immediately, at all speed—or else.

"Yo!" replied the Kid. "You'd best come take a look at him, Doc."

"There's times I wish I'd never started learning to be a

doctor," the slim Texan growled, but followed the Kid and Waco into the office.

Somehow, just how Galt could not decide, Dusty Fog appeared to have grown since his arrival. Walking towards the mayor at Mark Counter's side, the small Texan gave the impression of standing bigger than the blond giant.

"You can swear us in as soon as you like, Mayor," Dusty said. "And then I'll tell you just what I want doing."

Natural enemies tend to forget their differences in times of great common danger. When a forest fire rages, cougar and its natural prey, the whitetail deer, flee side by side; wolves and bears, incompatible at other times, swim to safety together; the prairie falcon and bobwhite quail settle alongside each other to rest tired wings after flying clear of the flames.

In much the same way the six men who had gathered in the private office of the Bella Union Saloon laid aside their past rivalries in the face of the present situation. Before the coming of Dusty Fog, all had been in serious and deadly competition for the right to pluck the golden Texas goose.

Eggars was host to the meeting, although none of the others realized it, having accepted the offer of the Bella Union's previous owner and bought the place subject to certain conditions being fulfilled. Tall, pale of skin as might be expected in a dude whose main activity came after sundown, he dressed almost to the height of current New York fashion. Strict arbiters of sartorial matters might have regarded his vest as just a touch loud, the gold watch chain across it maybe a mite ostentatious and the pearl in his cravat a wee bit too large, but his suit had been well-tailored and the mirror-surfaced boots made to his measure. Unless the other five, somewhat expert in that line, missed their guess, he was sitting at the head of the table unarmed. Certainly they saw no trace of concealed weapons on his person.

Bulky, sleepy-looking Jordan of the Blazing Pine sat

drumming thick, blunt fingers on the table top. In his shirt-sleeves, he dressed more like a bartender than the owner of a prosperous saloon. Despite his apparent lethargy, he was alert for treachery and carried a Colt thrust into his waist-band.

Next to Jordan, May of the May Day Music Hall rested the elbows of a loud check jacket upon the table. Red-faced, bald, with an expression of jovial good-fellowship permanently on his face, he clothed his medium-sized frame in violent clashes of color. In addition to operating a popular theater, he offered gambling and bed-mates to his customers. At no time did his right hand stray too far from the sleeve-holstered Remington Double Derringer.

Tall, sleek, elegantly attired after the manner of a range-country professional gambler, Bellamy of the First Chance Saloon sported a pearl-handled, nickel-plated Colt Civilian Peacemaker in a tied down fast-draw holster. His handsome face held an easy smile that did not go with the suspicious thoughts he harbored about the reason for the meeting.

Big, burly, scowling Will Burger, owner of the town's two highest-priced hog-ranches—brothels—showed less control of his feelings. Clearly suspicious, he leaned back in his chair with thumbs hooked on his jacket's lapels, the butt of a shoulder-holstered Merwin & Hulbert Army Pocket revolver displayed prominently.

Last of the party, and also the smallest of them, Coulton of the Good Fortune Gaming House shot interested glances about him. Lacking size or heft, he used brains and a shrewd judgment of human nature to control a place noted for the remarkable lack of good fortune its customers met with when playing the various gambling games. If that failed, he carried a Remington Double Derringer in his jacket pocket and was not averse to shooting through the cloth in the interests of surprise. Guessing that something of importance had brought about the gathering, he studied the others.

It was early in the evening on the day of Dusty Fog's explosive arrival. The small Texan had wasted no time in starting the work for which Governor Mansfield hired him. Much to Mayor Galt's dismay, Dusty demanded a civic ordinance authorizing the marshal to inspect every gambling device in town with the view of ensuring their honesty. After a brief attempt to delay the fatal document, hinting that a full assembly of the city fathers would be needed to create it, the mayor capitulated. Being a professional politician, Galt knew when he must surrender and exactly how far he dare go. At that moment in Trail End, Galt was working on a very short lunge-rein and feared it might curtail his liberty. So he produced the required ordinance and in a remarkably short time Dusty's deputies delivered copies of it around town.

Reading the full implications behind the new ruling, Eggars knew it would be war to the end. So he called a meeting of his chief competitors, the men most likely to possess the desire, contacts and means to deal with the threat to their continued prosperity. Realizing that he must temporarily stem their mistrust and rivalry, he arranged for the meeting to be held in the first-floor private office of the Bella Union. Before any of them could remark on the absence of its previous owner, Eggars brought their attention to the matter in hand.

"You've all heard, I reckon?"

"We've heard," Bellamy agreed. "What the hell's Galt doing to let it happen, damn him?"

"Galt's doing nothing, that's what!" Jordan spat out, seething with what—in him—passed as righteous indignation. "After all he's made out of m—us—he ought to—"

"Can you *prove* that he's ever taken a thin dime as a bribe?" interrupted Eggars. "I've tried, but he's got it all too well covered."

"Anyways, he can't do a thing against the Governor's orders," Coulton commented. "Galt's a full-time politician and that kind run scared real easy."

In common with the majority of his customers, May possessed a broad, raw sense of humor that demanded its entertainment be gamey and unrefined. So he could not hold down a raucous chuckle before saying:

"That's for sure. I bet he's sat to home right now, changing his drawers every time he hears anybody come to the front door."

Never had a piece of rough pleasantry met with such a lack of response. Not one of May's audience cracked so much as a smile. It had never been Jordan's way to pose as the gracious, jovial host and he refused to be diverted by any kind of facetiousness.

"So we sit back on our butt-ends and let those beef-head* bastards ruin us," he snorted. "That's bad business and damned poor sense."

"Did you read that civic ordinance Fog had Galt sign?" Bellamy asked.

"I'll say I did," admitted May, to whom the question had been directed. "It lets Fog do damn near everything except make mothers of us."

"You won't find it so damned funny when they start enforcing it," Jordan barked. "And don't go figuring they won't. Fog had the same game in Mulrooney. He worked it there."

"Could be that May reckons his theater'll carry him through," Coulton remarked, being all too aware of how the new ordinance would affect him.

"Maybe you're calling it right, Tom," Bellamy agreed, conscious of the fact that none of his equipment could stand inspection by a man wise in such matters. "May might even pick up business."

Annoyance flickered on May's face. "Word has it you're real good with that shiny pearl-handled gun, Bellamy. Why don't you call Fog out and settle it."

Sending his chair skidding backwards, Bellamy rose to

*Beef-head: derogatory name for a Texan.

stand with fingers spread over the Colt's butt.

"Any time you reckon I'm not *real* good, May, you just rear up on your hind legs and tell me."

"Now there's a real smart idea," Eggars put it hastily. "Let's all get a gun, go down into the street and shoot each other. That way we'll save Fog a whole heap of time and fuss."

"And what's that mean?" Bellamy demanded.

"That we've just one hope of licking Dusty Fog," Eggars replied, hand resting on the unopened leather cigar case lying before him. "By standing together. Unless we all forget we're after the same thing, or start remembering it, Fog'll have every last son of us headed out of town."

Slowly Bellamy relaxed and May sank back into his chair. Faced with the blunt truth, they saw it plainly enough. For the time being business rivalry and personal hostility must take a second place. When Bellamy resumed his seat at the table it seemed that peace had returned. The men looked at each other, savoring the feeling of peaceful co-existence and waiting for somebody to take the initiative.

"What we have to do is decide on how to get rid of those Texans," Eggars announced. "If all I've heard is true, we can't buy them off."

"I'd hate to be the one who tried it," May said dryly. "Knowed a feller who did, back when Fog run Mulrooney. He got kind of discouraged real quick."

"That being the case," Eggars continued, "we can either scare them off—"

"Happen you know anything that'll scare them, tell us what it is," Bellamy suggested.

"Have them fired," Eggars went on, ignoring the interruption. "Or kill them all."

Although the latter alternative struck the assembled company as being the one most likely to succeed, it bristled with difficulties. Every man present hired at least one member of his staff purely on ability with a gun; but none wished to chance losing his specialist while the others retained theirs.

"Just who're you figuring on doing the killing?" asked Coulton, putting the question in four other minds. "Unless you get them all first crack, Elwin's business'll sure be brisk—and not all of it from Texans."

"With Dusty Fog dead, the rest'll be easy," Eggars answered. "So we'll have him killed tonight."

"You are talking about *Dusty Fog,* aren't you?" Jordan asked.

"I am. Not that I intend to send somebody out to call him down on the main street in a fair fight."

"That'll be a real relief for *somebody,*" Bellamy stated.

"The man who tried it'd not be likely to come back," May went on.

"Just who've you got in mind?" demanded the ever blunt Jordan.

"Jackley," Eggars told them.

"Jackley!"

Five voices echoed the name, although none expressing a complimentary regard for the ex-marshal. Waiting until various comments on his choice had died down, Eggars explained his reasons for selecting Jackley as their instrument.

"He hates Fog's guts for what's happened at the jail and knows that he'll be run out of town again as soon as Fog hears he's snuck back. Besides which, he's stupid enough to think we'll put him back into office with Fog dead. And nobody'll connect him with us."

"Trouble being is he stupid enough to try killing Dusty Fog?" Bellamy asked.

"Stupid enough—or drunk enough, it's all one," Eggars assured him. "I've got him in the backroom downstairs liquored up and ready to go."

At which the others arrived at the point Eggars had hoped to avoid. He knew that it must be reached sooner or later, but hoped the delay would last as long as possible. Up to that moment the rest of the meeting had been too busy watching after their own interests to consider the matter of the missing proprietor of the saloon.

"You've got him—," Jordan repeated in a voice redolent of suspicion. "Where's Shipley?"

"He pulled out this afternoon, just after Fog rode in," Eggars explained, keeping his hand in the same deceptively casual manner upon the cigar case.

"And you glommed on to the Bella Union," May growled. "Damn it, I wanted a new place."

"So did I," Bellamy admitted.

"All right," Eggars said as he saw the mounting annoyance among the others. "If it'll keep the peace, I'll make you all a sporting proposition. If I don't get rid of Fog and the others, I'll let the man who does have this place for what it cost me."

"That sounds fair enough," Jordan remarked, a calculating glint in his eyes.

"You've got the odds on your side, Eggars," Bellamy stated. "But if you're betting on Jackley, I'll take cards."

"There's nothing to lose and plenty to gain," May said and began to shove back his chair. "Well, if that's all. I'll be on my way."

"Not yet, Sam," Eggars put in quietly. "We'll *all* stay here until after Jackley's made his play."

"You reckon I'd queer it?" demanded May, sounding as if the thought had never entered his head.

"Let's just say we're all good enough gamblers not to take chances," Eggars replied, taking up the cigar case but not opening it.

At first it seemed that May intended to argue, but he saw that four of the other five clearly backed Eggars' decision. Probably a similar idea has passed across each man's mind; but he decided that if he could not leave, nobody else must be given the opportunity.

"It's your play, Virg," May told Eggars sullenly and

there, it seemed, the matter would end.

So it might, but for one thing. All through the meeting Burger had sat silent and aware that the others merely tolerated him as a possible aid to their plans. Of all the men present, he stood to lose the least through the change of peace officers. In fact he might even gain by it. Rumor held that Dusty Fog took a tolerant attitude towards brothels, provided they ran in an orderly manner and without such profitable activities as rolling the clients. In addition to regarding brothels as a necessary evil, the small Texan took no bribes to allow their continued operation. So Burger did not wish to antagonize such an obliging man.

"You boys do what you want," he told the others. "I'm sitting out of it."

"It's not so easy as that, Burger," Eggars warned as the dissenter began to rise. "One in, all in's the way we play it."

"Then I'll change the rules!" Burger replied, right hand snapping across to disappear under the left side of his jacket.

Instantly, before any of the others could think of making a move, Eggars turned his hand towards the brothel-keeper. Just too late Burger noticed the hole in the end of the case and saw that a steel tube fitted into it. As Eggars pressed his thumb on a decorated stud in the center of the case's left side, flame spurted from the hole, and the sound of a light-caliber bullet igniting came from within.

For a moment shock twisted Burger's face, to be wiped off as a small, blue-rimmed hole suddenly formed in the center of his forehead. Death glazed his eyes and his body crashed to the floor with the revolver still held in the shoulder holster's grip.

Startled curses rose from Bellamy, May, Jordan and Coulton at the sight. Then they started to rise and froze as Eggars swung the wallet, smoke rising from the aperture, in an arc which took each of them in its sweep.

"There's four more bullets in it, gents," he said.

"What in hell's that thing?" May croaked, suddenly aware

that the case had been pointing his way a short time before.

"It's a Gaulois squeezer I picked up from a feller who bought it in Paris, France," Eggars replied. "Look outside and make sure that nobody heard the shot— Unless somebody wants to complain."

"I never did care for a mac," Bellamy commented. "Only folks're likely to ask how he died."

"We'll say that we got together to play cards, he cheated and got shot for it," Eggars answered. "I reckon you gents don't object to splitting the take of his two houses among us?"

"Times're going to be lean, unless we get rid of Fog," Coulton replied. "I always reckon that every bit helps."

Seeing that none of the others appeared inclined to take up the dead Burger's quarrel, Eggars relaxed. While Coulton checked that the shot had not been overheard, Eggars condescended to show the others the secret of the gun which had caused it.

With the case open, he took out a strange-looking gun. In appearance it resembled a short-barreled, single-shot pistol with a square butt and no trigger as such. However the Gaulois held five 8 mm bullets in a magazine much like the one used in the Mauser automatic pistols that would come along in the future. Instead of a trigger, squeezing the operating stud fed a cartridge into the chamber and fired it, while on being released the working parts ejected the empty case to make way for the next round.

The Gaulois was not an automatic pistol in the sense that later weapons, using the force of the recoil to operate the mechanism, would be. Light of weight, not more than five-eighths of an inch thick, it could be easily carried without making a bulge in the pocket noticeable to trained eyes. Or, disguised in some manner, it offered an unsuspected means of defense.

"Let's get things ready," Eggars ordered, after being assured that the sound of the shot had passed unnoticed and satisfying the others' curiosity about the nature of his hide-out weapon. "We'll want cards, money, everything set up ready."

"That's easy arranged," Coulton replied.

"Then let's get it done," ordered Eggars. "And as soon as we're ready, cut loose a shot with a Derringer one of you. We want something that will be heard to get folks up here."

When Dusty heard of the shooting, he and Mark visited the saloon. Everything appeared to point to the truth of the story told by Eggars' party. Knowing that no matter what had really happened, he would be unlikely to be able to prove it, Dusty let the men think he accepted the affair as a shooting in self-defense during a poker game. So he contented himself with warning that the inspection of the various gambling games would take place in the morning and left.

"So that's the smart Captain Fog, is it," grinned Eggars, collecting his money. "He took it like a bigmouth bass grabbing a minnow in spring."

"I wish I'd your confidence," Coulton replied, picking up the Derringer with which the other claimed to have killed Burger.

"He didn't ask many questions," Bellamy went on. "Could be he believed us."

"What do you reckon, Dusty?" Mark asked as they left the saloon.

"The shooting happened near enough the way they told it."

"Only?"

"Only I don't see them six yahoos gathering for a poker game today of all days. Do you?"

"Nope," Mark admitted. "I'd've thought they'd be cleaning their places up, or maybe gathered to decide how they'd get rid of us."

"Which's likely what got them together," Dusty guessed. "Only Burger didn't want to stay in with them."

"He ran the hog-ranches, didn't he?"

"Some of them. Likely he figured he'd got less to lose with us here. They daren't chance him going out and telling us what they planned, so they made sure he couldn't."

"Do you reckon that Eggars shot him?"

"Sure. None of them would take the blame for one of the others. Eggars made wolf-bait of him all right—only not with that Derringer."

"That wasn't a .41 hole," Mark agreed. "Why lie about the gun he used?"

"Likely he had a good reason," Dusty answered. "I've got a chore for Doc—and he's not going to like it."

Guessing what the chore would be, Mark nodded soberly. "So what do we do next?" he asked.

"Wait to learn what *they're* fixing to do."

"Kill you for starters," the blond giant guessed. "They know they can't scare you out, or buy you off. So it has to be that way."

"Why sure," Dusty replied, showing a remarkable lack of concern. "And real soon, or I miss my guess. Let's go back to the office so's I can tell Doc what I want for him to do."

"It's time for you to start," Eggars told Jackley, entering the backroom of the Bella Union saloon with a shotgun across the crook of his arm. "Fog's just left on his rounds of the town, and he's alone."

Slowly the former marshal of Trail End raised his face and stared through bleary eyes. Hearing that the time had come filled him with mixed feelings. Pain still throbbed at his body from the beating taken at Dusty's hands. Thinking of the easy life that could not return while the small Texan lived gave him an added incentive to carry on. Fed by careful controlled quantities of whiskey his rage remained, but all traces of caution had fled.

"I'll fix him," Jackley promised thickly.

"Here," Eggars replied, laying the shotgun on the table.

"Wha's that for?"

"You're figuring on trying to take him with your bare hands again, maybe?"

"I tol' you," Jackley muttered. "There was four of 'em—"

"And I believe you," Eggars sniffed. "Just as long as you make sure that you hit the right one."

"Don't you worry none about that. As soon as he walks by here—"

"Not here!" Eggars interrupted hurriedly. "Lay for him in the alley between the theater and the Chinese laundry. They're both closed for the night and Fog'll have to come by them on his way to the office."

"That's where I'll do it from," Jackley said. "Lemme have another drink."

"When you're through," Eggars answered and saw anger twist the coarse face. "There's not time to send for another bottle now, you might miss him on the street."

Probably the latter consideration weighed most heavily in favor of Jackley's acceptance. "You have one ready for when I come back," he ordered and lurched to his feet.

Eggars watched anxiously, wondering if he might have been too liberal in the supply of liquor. For a moment Jackley stood swaying, but steadied himself and picked up the shotgun. Then he walked across the room to the door which opened on the bar.

"Not that way!" Eggars snapped, but once again softened his tone. "We don't want word to get out to Fog that you're back in town, do we?"

"Naw!" Jackley agreed with some warmth. "I don't."

Going to the other door, Eggars opened it and looked along the passage leading to the saloon's rear entrance. Satisfied that there was nobody around to see the ex-marshal's departure, he escorted Jackley to the back door. Once more the saloonkeeper looked out and, finding the rear devoid of witnesses, turned to his dupe.

"Go to it."

"Don't you forget that bottle when I get back."

"It'll be waiting," Eggars promised and closed the door.

Shotgun under arm, Jackley slouched away from the Bella Union. While far from an intelligent man, he possessed sufficient reasoning power to stay off the main street. As Eggars had pointed out, the work in hand would be sufficiently dangerous without adding to it by warning Dusty Fog of his presence in town. So he stuck to the back streets, but took no precautions beyond that.

To hear Eggars talk, public opinion was solidly against Dusty Fog being marshal of Trail End and the man who removed him would be hailed as a civic benefactor. So Jackley felt that anybody who saw and recognized him would understand that he was going to perform a necessary task for the town's welfare. With the small Texan dead, the other four could be arrested or run out of town, and the good old days resume once more.

The time was close to midnight and the town quiet. During the afternoon Dusty had visited each trail crew around the area. By hard persuasion and a clear statement of how he stood, he had managed to quiet down the explosive situation. Remembering how he had run Mulrooney, the other Texans were prepared to wait and see what differences his assumption of office made to conditions in Trail End. So the night passed quietly, few of the saloons offering gambling and all holding down on the kind of mistreatment which had caused so much trouble in the days when Jackley wore the marshal's badge.

By the time Jackley started on his mission of murder, almost all the town's businesses had closed. On main street only a few lights glowed where swampers cleaned up, or sweating, cursing men worked to make a variety of gambling devices suitable for inspection. From glances taken between buildings, Jackley saw that the main street was almost devoid of pedestrians or traffic. He regarded it as an omen, or a tribute to himself from the citizens, leaving the way for him to carry out his task.

Although Jackley did not know it, a Trail End citizen

saw him slouching along, noted the shotgun and guessed at his mission. Even if he had known it, his drink-soddened mind would have found no cause for concern. All evening suggestions of the high regard the townsfolk held him in had been drummed into his thick skull, cemented there along with his hatred of Dusty Fog by Old Whipping Post. So he went his way unseeing and uncaring.

Reaching the theater he found it and the Chinese laundry in darkness. Before passing along the wide alley separating the buildings, he drew back the gun's two hammers to full cock. With that precaution taken, he moved cautiously along to where he could see the street. Across and slightly below where he stood, the marshal's office glowed with light and the big shape of Mark Counter passed before the left side window. Maybe after dropping Dusty Fog, Jackley could down the blond giant; but the small Texan must die first.

Perhaps if Jackley had been given time to stand and brood, he might have become worried. No man reached the prominence Dusty Fog achieved in *pistolero* circles unless fully capable of defending himself fast and skillfully. Allowed time to remember the nature of his victim, the ex-marshal might have wondered if the proposed murder would be so simple as Eggars promised. The required time was not granted.

Along the street boot heels thumped upon the sidewalk. Peeking carefully around the corner of the theater, Jackley saw the small shape of his enemy approaching on the other side. A low hiss of satisfaction left Jackley's lips at the sight. It seemed that Eggars had spoken the truth, for Dusty walked alone, apparently unaccompanied by any of the deputies.

A more able lawman than Jackley might have wondered at Dusty's solo condition. However the ex-marshal found nothing unusual in the sight. Never having had the services of a deputy, he felt no suspicions. Thinking of his own methods of law enforcement, his only thoughts on the matter stemmed from Dusty's eccentric behavior in bothering to make the rounds at all. However the peculiar habits of the small Texan made Jackley's work that much easier. Going into the office after him would have been fraught with danger.

So, not wishing to look a gift-horse too closely in the mouth—in case it proved to be a grizzly bear in disguise—he accepted his good luck and prepared to capitalize on it. He felt neither fear nor remorse at what he meant to do. Whiskey dampened the first and the second was foreign to his nature. In his hands he gripped the ideal weapon for his purpose. Nine buckshot balls, each .32 in caliber, spreading across the street could hardly miss. Turning loose all eighteen from both barrels would render it even less likely to happen.

Nearer came the sound of approaching feet, making that distinctive thunking peculiar to high-heeled cowhand footwear. Jackley swung the shotgun up, making sure that it did not catch against the wall and give out a warning noise. Cuddling the butt against his shoulder, he looked along the rib between the two barrels. Already the hammers sat at the full-cock position and his finger was curled around the trigger. Across the street Dusty Fog came into sight, strolling along without a suspicion of peril. Nothing could save the small Texan—

Then suddenly, shockingly loud and terrifyingly plain, a voice rang out from the darkness at the rear of the buildings.

"Watch out, Cap'n Fog!" it cried.

While the prospect of setting himself up as a target did not appeal to Dusty, he knew it must be done if he hoped to bring his enemies into the open. Accepting the unpleasant fact that somebody would most probably try to kill him that night, before he could impress honest citizens with his fairness and competence, he gave thought to minimizing the risk.

Not for a moment did he think evicting the former marshal would end the affair. There were too many people in Trail End—the five he saw at the Bella Union prominent among them—who had no desire to see law and order rigidly enforced. They would not hesitate to try to kill him. If they did not make the attempt themselves, there were plenty willing to take the chore for money. Well, considering the reputation of the victim, not plenty; but enough to make life real interesting, if short, given half a good chance.

So Dusty did not intend to present the opportunity.

Although he apparently left the office alone, he knew that the Kid had gone out by the rear door. All the time Dusty was parading around town in plain view, the Kid was hovering in the background, a rifle-armed, deadly silent shadow watching his back and ready to take cards should the need arise.

The time passed slowly, with nothing to relieve the monotony of making the rounds. At last Dusty decided that he had given his enemies enough of a chance for one night, so he directed his feet towards the marshal's office. Maybe the unprecedented early hour of closing practiced by most of the town's places of entertainment heralded some form of trouble. The owners might be trying to lull him into a sense of false security. Or perhaps they wanted as much time as possible to put their houses in order. Across the street, the theater lay black, deserted, with an extra dead look after the lights and gaiety it had given out all evening. Next door, the staff of the Chinese laundry must all be in bed, for no sign of activity came from within. Once at the office, he could sit back and relax, providing he stayed away from lighted windows.

Two things saved Dusty when the shouted warning reached his ears.

Hearing the unexpected intervention so shocked Jackley that he jumped nervously, causing the shotgun's barrels to lift as he jerked its forward trigger.

That was the first item which helped to keep Dusty Fog alive, the second being his superbly lightning fast reactions.

At the first word his head swiveled around and he saw a shape blacker than the surrounding darkness of the alley across the street. By that time he had already started moving, going forward into a rolling dive calculated to carry him off the sidewalk, with hands crossing to the butts of his guns. When the shotgun's first barrel belched out its load, its upwards movement and Dusty's dive combined to carry him just past the deadly spreading pattern of the balls.

Landing on his shoulder, Dusty rolled over to his stomach and cut loose with two shots. Already the Kid was bounding along the sidewalk across the street. No boots covered his feet and the *Pehnane* moccasins he wore allowed him to move with the deadly silence of a charging jaguar.

Lead whistled by Jackley's head, coming from Dusty's Colts. Still inflamed by the raw whiskey, the ex-marshal knew no caution. Wild with rage at Dusty for daring to spoil his careful plans, Jackley lunged forward and tried to re-line the shotgun on his victim. In doing so, he made the mistake of emerging from the cover of the end of the theater.

Skidding to a halt, the Kid went into action. From waist high, shooting by instinctive alignment, the deadly Winchester spat flame and lead. Four times, as fast as he could work the lever and squeeze the trigger, the Kid fired. Each time a two hundred grain, flat-nosed .44.40 bullet ripped into Jackley's body. The first knocked him off balance and the rest completed the work. Although the shotgun's second barrel spewed buckshot, the balls went nowhere near their intended mark. Letting the gun drop, Jackley collided with the wall of the laundry. He hung there for a moment, then sank down into a sitting position.

Cautiously, guns held ready for use, Dusty and the Kid converged on Jackley. Mark burst out of the office carrying a shotgun and lights began to show, or heads appear at windows.

"Who is it?" Dusty asked, still half-blinded by the

muzzle-blast of his Colts.

Having been standing erect, with his rifle's barrel held well below the line of sight, the Kid suffered less from the glow burning powder gave out in darkness. So he could make out enough of the would-be murderer to guess at the man's identity.

"That Jackley *hombre,*" he replied. "The damned fool must've got off the train somewhere down the track and come back looking for you."

"He found me," Dusty said quietly, peering along the alley in the hope of seeing his unknown benefactor.

"Who was it that yelled?" asked the Kid, following the direction of Dusty's gaze.

"I don't know."

"Want for me to go take a look?"

Quickly Dusty balanced the issues involved in the suggestion. No sign of the shouter showed, nor sound to say that he remained or intended to come for an expression of gratitude. Clearly whoever gave the warning did not mean to make himself known. If he possessed some ulterior motive for the intervention, he would make sure of not being found. Should he have acted out of friendship, or a desire to see a clean-up of Trail End, he might pay for his action with his life. It would be mighty poor thanks to discover the identity of the friend, but cause his death. There could, of course, be only one answer.

"Leave him be, Lon. If he's a friend, we can use every one that comes our way."

"You all right, Dusty?" Mark asked, coming up.

"He missed me clean," the small Texan replied, rasping a match on the seat of his pants.

"Wonder where he got the scatter," the Kid remarked, studying the weapon in the match's glow. "He for sure didn't have it when we put him on the train."

Bending down, Dusty picked the weapon up. "See to

things here, Lon," he said and walked towards the office.

In the better illumination Dusty examined the shotgun. It proved to be one of the twenty-inch barrel Greeners that Wells Fargo supplied to their messengers. Almost new, it showed a greater amount of care than had been lavished on the weapons racked upon the office wall.

"That's a real good gun, Dusty," Mark commented, following him inside and watching the examination.

"Sure," the small Texan replied. "Sold through Keever & Grayle in Chicago."

"Maybe Ed Ballinger can find out who bought it," Mark suggested.

"That's just what I was thinking," Dusty answered.

Shortly after running the law in Mulrooney, back in the Rio Hondo, the floating outfit found themselves helping a Chicago policeman capture a criminal who had fled to Texas.* Detective Lieutenant Ed Ballinger never forgot the friendship, cooperation and training in gun-handling he received from the Texans. As on the last occasion when Dusty requested assistance,† Ballinger would do his best to supply it.

If Ballinger could establish ownership of the shotgun, it might lead to the man who put Jackley up to the attempted murder. Dusty doubted if the ex-marshal owned the gun, its condition showed too much care and attention for that. So somebody gave it to him, primed him with whiskey—not even death could remove the raw smell of liquor from him—and sent him on the mission of death. Once Dusty knew the man's identity, he could plan to counter other such attempts.

"I'll get the message off first thing in the morning," Mark said.

*Told in *The Law of the Gun*.
† Told in *The Fortune Hunters*.

"Do that," Dusty replied, then looked up as Waco and Doc entered the office from the living quarters at the rear. "It's all over, go back to bed. You've got a hard day's work comes morning."

After his deputies had retired for the night, Dusty lay on his bed and looked up at the roof. The first attempt to remove him from office had failed. It would not be the last. With that thought, he turned on to his side and went to sleep.

PART TWO

Jordan's Try

"I tell you that I bought them damned cards in good faith!" Lou Jordan insisted, with such vehemence that he might almost have been speaking the truth. "I didn't know they was marked!"

Considering that some twenty new decks of cards lay on the pile to which Doc Leroy objected, the saloonkeeper's faith appeared at the best misplaced.

By working through the night, Jordan's staff had removed various appliances attached to gambling equipment with the intention of reducing to a minimum the danger of a customer winning. Although he could not entirely obliterate traces of such appliances' presence, the fact that they no longer remained to halt a wheel or control the fall of dice proved his sterling motives—or at least prevented any chance of proving he made use of them.

In addition he had replaced all the brace boxes of his faro layouts with the legitimate variety slotted so that only one card, not two at the discretion of the dealer, could pass.

Realizing that "Sand-Tell" decks, with the high cards sanded to a smooth finish on their faces and the low cards on their backs, or "belly-strippers"* could be easily detected, he disposed of a good collection of both kinds. However the salesman from the gambling supply house had sworn that the decks of "readers", marked cards, could only be detected by somebody who knew the secret code worked into the design on the backs.

Jordan learned, too late, that gambling supply houses, like legitimate business companies, tended towards exaggeration in their advertising claims.

Holding each deck in turn in his left hand, Doc riffled them rapidly with his other thumb. While an honest design remained steady to the eye, the alteration of the pattern caused by the marks to denote rank or suit did not. With such a guide, Doc selected the "readers" from their "twins"; the honest decks with back designs matching those of the "readers".

"Didn't, huh?" Dusty said unsympathetically.

"How could Mr. Jordan suspect when the revenue tax stamps were on the packets?" put in a florid-face, impressive-looking man coming forward.

"Who're you?" Dusty asked bluntly, although he knew.

"Cyrus F. Grosvenor, attorney-at-law, acting for Mr. Jordan—"

"Did he figure he'd need you, counselor?" Doc inquired, looking the soberly and expensively attired man over from head to toe.

"I—I just happened to be here on another matter," Grosvenor replied. "Mr. Jordan requested my presence as a precaution."

"Against what?" Dusty demanded.

"The detection of dishonest gambling equipment requires a specialized knowledge, marshal," Grosvenor answered,

*For a description of "belly-strippers" read *Calamity Spells Trouble*.

clearly feeling out his words. "Mr. Jordan expressed a justifiable curiosity as to whether any of your deputies possessed such knowledge."

"And do I?" Doc wanted to know.

"You seem remarkably competent, deputy."

"That's a whole lot of good faith," Dusty remarked, indicating the heap of marked decks.

"You say they'd all got their stamps on!" Jordan protested hotly. "How the hell was I to know— Hey! Maybe somebody figured to come here and cheat folks, or me, with them marked decks they snuck in."

Not a bad afterthought, Jordan mused, presenting him in the light of a potential victim to some plot. Watching the two Texans, he could see no sign that they believed or rejected his words.

"Where'd you get your cards, Mr. Jordan?" Dusty asked.

"From a traveling salesman."

"He totes along that many decks?"

"Naw. They're shipped here from Chicago by the company he works for."

"Who are the folks he works for?"

"Huh?" grunted Jordan, not caring for the way the conversation developed. When making his suggestion, it had not been with the intention of involving the gambling supply house.

"May I ask, as Mr. Jordan's attorney, the reason for that question, marshal?" Grosvenor put in, realizing the saloonkeeper could not think up a suitable answer and hoping to prevent the need arising.

"Like your client says," Dusty drawled. "Somebody could've been fixing to use them marked cards. If they snuck that many in, there has to be a reason. So I'd like to catch whoever it is. It being my job to protect honest citizens."

Grosvenor read no hint of sarcasm on Dusty's face. What the lawyer realized was that he had been driven into a corner. After making such a suggestion, Jordan must give answers or arouse suspicion—or rather confirm it, for Grosvenor doubted if Dusty believed a word the saloonkeeper said.

"Will knowing where they came from help?" the lawyer asked.

"Maybe, counselor. Lieutenant Ed Ballinger of the Chicago police and me're *amigos*. When I telegraph asking him for help, he'll give it."

The fame of Detective Lieutenant Ed Ballinger had spread as far west as Kansas' railroad towns. Being a lawyer who specialized in keeping dishonest men out of the law's grasp, Grosvenor had better cause than most people to know it. In addition to fighting crime in Chicago, Ballinger was the officer who went to Texas after the Big Man, Anthony Reckharts. Thinking back, Grosvenor recollected that Dusty Fog had played a major part in assisting Ballinger to dispose of the master criminal. So the small Texan was not bluffing when he claimed Ballinger's friendship. Clearly the time had come for frank speech and public spirit.

"As your legal adviser, Mr. Jordan," Grosvenor said with great emphasis, "I suggest that you give the marshal the information he requires."

"Gi—!" Jordan began, then chopped off his words. The lawyer always steered his clients right. It seemed that somebody must be sacrificed. Tough luck, but necessary. "It's the Sheppey Novelty Company on Forty-fifth Street."

"And Lieutenant Ballinger'll find them there?"

"That's where they are," Jordan agreed sullenly.

"You get much stuff from Chicago, Mr. Jordan?"

"Some."

"From Keever and Grayle?"

"There and other places."

"I hear tell they sell good guns," Dusty said.

"Could be," Jordan answered noncommittally. "I never bought one from them."

"I'm through now, Dusty," Doc said, sweeping the "readers" into the gunny-sack he had brought along for the purpose. "It's good to see that you run such a straight place, Mr. Jordan."

If looks could kill, Trail End would have needed a new marshal and gambling-expert deputy from that moment. Raw fury twisted Jordan's face as he contemplated a future spent operating with honest equipment. True the house percentage would continue to draw in its inevitable profit, but nowhere near that guaranteed by the crooked gear; and with the awful possibility of players walking out winning.

"Let's go, Doc," Dusty drawled, holding down a grin. "We'll be looking over the First Chance after dinner, counselor, in case you've any business with *its* owner."

Before the lawyer could think up an adequate reply, Dusty and Doc turned to walk away. Jordan's face turned almost purple with held-down emotions and his hand went towards the butt of the revolver in his waistband.

"Don't be a fool!" Grosvenor hissed in alarm. "That's not the answer—or this isn't the time for it. You'll just ha—"

The words died away as the lawyer saw a man step into the saloon and block the two Texans' path.

"Well I'll be—," the newcomer began in a cultured deep South drawl. "If it's not young Marvin Leroy. How are you-all, boy?"

"Fit as frog's hair, Joe," Doc replied, extending his hand as the man set down the carpetbag he carried. "Dusty, this here's my old friend Joe Brambile."

From the white Stetson on his head to the well-polished boots gracing his feet, Joe Brambile looked every inch a very successful Southern plantation owner of the days when cotton ruled as king. Hair greying at the temples lent dignity to a thin, aristocratic face with a moustache and goatee beard so neat that they might just have been trimmed by a master barber. His lean frame set off the cutaway coat, frilly-bosomed shirt and string tie in a manner to gladden a tailor's heart, while the tight legged trousers bore sharp creases.

"I've heard of you, Mr. Brambile," Dusty remarked, shaking hands with the man after Doc had completed the ritual. His voice held less warmth than might be expected when meeting an old friend of his deputy.

Despite his distinguished, almost venerable, appearance, Joe Brambile's sole connection with deep South plantations came from playing cards with their owners on Mississippi riverboats before the War. A professional gambler, he had a reputation for skill, ability and luck; with hints that on occasion luck had been improved by manipulation of the pasteboards.

Dusty realized that any successful professional gambler gathered such stories from losers jealous of his success. Yet he wished that Doc had met Brambile in a less public place. Sensing the interest that the greetings caused, Dusty knew that he and Doc might come to regret the latter showing friendship to a man like the gambler.

Already Doc had displayed his ability to detect crooked gambling devices and people could be wondering where he had gained his knowledge. Dishonest gamblers did not broadcast their secrets, so there might be an erroneous significance attached to Doc being aware of such things. Dusty knew his deputy to be completely honest, but others might refuse to accept him in that light due to his friendship with Brambile.

"I surely hope that you-all heard something good, sir," Brambile said.

"You staying in town?" Dusty asked, evading the question.

"That depends, sir, on how the action is."

"It's real slow right now."

"In Trail End, sir? Wildest and most wide open of all the cattle-drive towns?"

"They do say that's just a rumor started by folks in Dodge City, Joe," Doc put in. "Where're you staying?"

"As always at the place which most merits my custom," Brambile answered, apparently unmoved by Dusty's lack of cordiality.

"That means the Elite Plaza Hotel," Doc grinned, taking

in the obvious signs of Brambile's affluence. "I'll walk down there with you."

"See you're wearing a badge, boy. Don't you have work to do?"

"Not until after dinner," Doc replied. "Unless you want me for anything right now, Dusty."

For a moment Dusty felt tempted to say they would inspect the First Chance Saloon's gambling equipment before dinner. Then he put the thought aside. Already he had gone further than he liked in his show of disapproval.

"No, you go ahead," he said. "I'll meet you at the First Chance after I've eaten."

"Something tells me that Captain Fog doesn't like me, Marvin, me boy," the gambler remarked as he and Doc walked along the street towards the best of the town's three hotels.

"He's got one hell of a stinking chore here," Doc replied. "In Quiet Town and Mulrooney at least he had the honest folks backing him. Not here."

"They do say this's a bad town," Brambile admitted. "Fast, high and bad."

"That's what they say, Joe. One thing, though. I took an oath with this tin star and I'll keep it."

"I'd expect you to."

"Stay out of trouble, Joe," Doc warned soberly.

"Me boy, you know nobody's ever once proved that I've cheated," Brambile grinned and touched his side with his left hand. "There's some who've tried to, mind."

In the saloon, Jordan let out a long string of spluttering curses the moment the Texans left.

"I never figured they'd have anybody as slick as that pale-faced bastard," he snarled and glared at his floor manager who was hovering in the background. "How about seeing they don't keep him, Mitch?"

Tall, lean, hard-faced Mitch Tatem showed no enthusiasm and some alarm at the suggestion. "That's Doc Leroy, boss. They do say he's near on as fast as Dusty Fog. It was him who took out Killrain, the Hired Butcher, last year."*

Which meant that Doc Leroy ranked among the top names of the fast-draw fraternity, Killrain having been a paid killer noted for his speed with a gun. However Jordan felt disinclined to be swayed from his purpose.

"Can't you get him anyways? There'll be a hundred simoleons in it for you."

"I wouldn't advise you to try it," Grosvenor put in. "At least not without certain preparations."

"Such as?" Jordan demanded.

"Such as making sure that the good citizens of this town—and there are some around—"

"Like the son-of-a-bitch who warned Fog last night?"

"For one, Lou, there're more—"

"Let 'em watch to themselves, I say," growled the saloonkeeper.

"That can come later," Grosvenor answered. "Let's make sure first that the good citizens lose faith in those Texans. Right now there're plenty of folks sat on the fence, just ready to jump down at Fog's side if it looks like he can win. If we can discredit Leroy, it'll be a damned good start to breaking the others."

"So how do we do it?"

"Those cattle-buyers and trail bosses still like to play poker. High stake stud, too. They'll be even more eager to play now Leroy and Fog've given your gear a clean bill of health."

"You're still way ahead of me."

"Brambile likes the same kind of game. If he hears that one's going, he'll be along to sit in. With him and Leroy being such good friends, things could be arranged. It's a pity they took all your 'readers'."

*Told in *The Hard Riders*.

"They ain't got 'em all," Tatem put in. "I've a couple of decks in my room."

"We'll only need the one," Grosvenor stated. "Just as long as the big game gets a deck of 'twins'. See to that and play it this way—"

Listening to the lawyer, Jordan saw the plan offered a means to remove at least one threat to his prosperity. In addition to leaving the way open for Dusty Fog's dismissal, it opened up the prospects of returning to the old methods of operating the gambling games.

"Psst! Cap'n Fog!" hissed a voice, bringing Dusty and Doc to a halt. Turning with hands fanning to gun butts, they looked in the direction of the speaker.

The small man stood well back in the alley alongside a general store, keeping to where the evening shadows lay darkest and exhibiting all the alert nervousness of a much-hunted pronghorn antelope. Going closer, Doc formed the impression that he neither washed nor shaved to excess and appeared to sleep regularly in his clothes, not in the cleanest of beds. Constantly darting glances behind him, the man flashed the Texans a gap-toothed grin.

"Howdy, Mousey," Dusty greeted. "I didn't think this'd be your kind of town."

"I've been around since I heard you was coming in to run the law, Cap'n," the man answered, still showing his teeth in an ingratiating manner.

"So what do you know?"

"Not much. Just a whisper I heard this afternoon. There's a big game at the Blazing Pine tonight. Word has it that Jordan's brought in a sharper called Joe Brambile to cheat for the house."

"Why you—!" Doc began, moving forward with such an expression of fury that Mousey backed up against the wall in alarm.

"Easy, Doc!" Dusty ordered. "Mousey's doing no more than telling us what he's heard."

"Hell yes, friend," the little man put in hastily. "I don't know whether it's true or not. I'm only saying what the word is."

Hovering on the fringes of the outlaw element, Mousey acted as messenger and go-between. In addition he sold some of the information that came his way to the law. On hearing that the Governor had brought Dusty in to tame Trail End, the little man traveled to the town. Mousey guessed that there might be good pickings, with little risk, and the news he just gave Dusty was the first to come along. Yet it seemed to annoy the slim deputy and Mousey wondered why.

"Here," Dusty said, holding out a five dollar bill.

"Thankee, Cap'n!" Mousey replied, taking the money and stuffing it into his pocket in a single movement. "Anything special you want to know?"

"Sure. Find out who liquored Jackley up and primed him to come after me."

"There's some say it was Sam May."

"Is that what you say?" Dusty asked, having faith in the little informer's judgment."

"Naw!" Mousey snorted. "If he had, he'd've put Jackley next to one of the other places. Having him try alongside the theater'd be like peeing on your own door-step."

Which just about coincided with Dusty's own views. Having met May that afternoon while examining the theater's gambling equipment, Dusty doubted if the man had the type of mentality to play a double bluff by ordering the attempt from outside his own premises. So Dusty brought up another point of interest.

"Who's taken over Burger's hog-ranches?"

"Dunno," Mousey admitted.

"Find out," Dusty ordered.

"That could run into money—"

"You've just made five dollars for something that'll likely come to nothing," Dusty growled. "That's more than enough to spend in a joy-house. They do say too much of it weakens a man."

"I'll see what I can learn," Mousey promised and scuttled off towards the rear of the buildings.

"Let's go, Doc," Dusty said, but the other did not move. "Come on. I don't want folks to see Mousey going out of here and us stood in it."

"The lousy lil skunk!" Doc spat out, still looking to where the little man disappeared. "I don't give a whoop in hell what happens to him."

"I do!" Dusty stated grimly. "He's not the cleanest, or best-looking cuss you'll meet, but he's been mighty useful to me. And I figure that if I pay to use what he risks getting killed to learn, I've no right to cause him grief."

With that Dusty turned and walked back to the main street. For a moment Doc stood glaring after the departed Mousey, then followed. For a time he and Dusty walked in silence, but as they approached the office Doc broke it.

"You reckon he's telling the truth about Joe, don't you?"

"Mousey knows me better than to make up news. If he heard it, he'd tell me."

"But you reckon it's true about Joe!" Doc insisted.

"How long've you known me, Doc?" Dusty inquired gently.

"A fair few years, ever since Quiet Town."

"Like you say, a fair few years."

"Sure."

"Did you ever in that time know me to decide something I heard was true without checking it out myself?"

"You don't," Doc admitted. "Only I've seen you friendlier than this morning when we met Joe."

"I'll go with you on that. Right then and there was just about the worst damned time for you to meet up with him."

"Joe's a straight gambler!" Doc growled. "Hell, Dusty,

I've heard folks claim Frank Derringer's a shark, but he was your deputy in Mulrooney, doing what I'm handling here."

"Sure," Dusty agreed, guessing what was coming next.

"You trusted Frank—"

"I *know* Frank," Dusty pointed out.

"And I know Joe Brambile—maybe better than you know Frank Derringer," Doc stated. "Most of the things you're using came from him."

By that time they had reached the office and entered. Mark and Waco sat at the desk, but they rose and both looked at Doc as he followed Dusty inside. One glance at Mark and the youngster told Dusty that they had grave, important matters on their minds.

"Heard the word, Dusty?" Mark asked.

"What about?"

"There's a big game tonight at the Blazing Pine—"

"We've heard," Dusty agreed.

"And the rest?" Mark said quietly, eyes flickering to Doc.

"What's the rest?" the slim deputy demanded.

"That Joe Brambile's playing for the house—and how he's a real good friend of yours."

"Damn it, Mark!" Waco blazed. "You should've let me bust that son-of-a-bitching bardog's face in for the way he said it."

"Which'd only make it look like what he hinted at was true," Mark told him.

"What did he say?" Doc demanded.

"That word had it we didn't aim to enforce the gambling law all the way—for some folks," Mark replied.

"Which bardog said it?" Doc spat out.

"It doesn't matter which one," Dusty put in.

"The hell it doesn't!" Doc shouted, anger working on his pallid face. "I aim to—"

"Go out there and do just like somebody wants you to do," Dusty interrupted gently but firmly. "I'll give them one thing, they've worked fast. Mark, go find Mousey—

he's in town—arrest him for being drunk and bring him in. Take Waco with you in case he shows fight."

"Yo!" Mark answered, giving the old cavalry assent and knowing that Waco would not be accompanying him to help bring in the little informer. Then, when the youngster hesitated, growled, "I don't want to have to carry you, boy."

"Damn it all!" Waco objected. "Can't I—?"

"No you can't," Dusty replied. "Go help Mark."

Swinging on his heel, the youngster stamped angrily out of the office after the blond giant. A faint smile crossed Dusty's face as he watched the indignant departure. Then he spun on his heel, tossed his Stetson across to the hook by the door and sat at the desk.

"Boy looks a mite riled," he said. "Rest your feet, Doc. A man can always talk and think straighter with something solid under his butt-end. And for Pete's sake stop thinking I'm just looking for ways to run Joe Brambile out of Trail End. Can't you see what's happening?"

"Sure," Doc agreed, taking the chair at the other side of the desk. "Both me and Joe's being made look bad."

"If it doesn't happen again while you're wearing a badge, you'll be more lucky than most," Dusty said. "Thing being now, not who's doing it, but how do we stop them getting away with it?"

"Waco reckons he knows a way," Doc remarked.

"He's young enough to still reckon a fist in the mouth'll stop it talking."

"It's nice to know you reckon I'm all old and worn out," Doc said in a much milder tone. "You reckon there's something behind this rumor?"

"I *know* there is," Dusty stated. "Everything's falling just a shade too pat. Do you know why Joe Brambile came into the Blazing Pine?"

"To see what the chance of some action might be."

"Just how well do you know him, Doc?"

Sensing that something far more than idle curiosity prompted the question, Doc felt no resentment at it. He knew just how delicate their position in Trail End was. Governor Mansfield had not hidden the fact that there had been opposition to his selection of Texans to run the law in the town. So Doc wished to avoid jeopardizing Dusty's chances to success.

"Real well," he replied. "Maybe twelve years back, just afore I went East to the medical school, pappy stitched a tear in his side that some feller gave him in a poker game. Joe near on died, and it came out that the other feller had been doing the cheating. Anyways, Joe stayed at our place while he could travel. It was then he started to teach me about gambling. Said he figured a student ought to know more than book-learning happen he was going to stay in a big city, and that I should know what to watch out for."

"He taught you well," Dusty complimented.

"Him, and other gamblers he passed word to," Doc answered. "But that's not the reason I'm beholden to Joe."

"Why else?"

"He helped me when I went after the three men who killed pappy in the fuss over the water-rights back to home."

While Dusty knew that Doc's return from medical school stemmed from his father's death during a feud over ownership of water-rights, he had never heard the full story. All Dusty remembered of the affair was that Doc's father had taken three bullets as he went to tend to a wounded man, being shot by members of the other faction in the feud. That brought an end to Doc's education. Returning to Texas, he strapped on a Colt and went out to avenge his father.

"I could easily have gone bad, but for Joe," Doc said, after giving Dusty the bare details of the shooting and his return. "The fellers who shot pappy belonged to what came out as the winning side, which put them on top in the county. Anyways the three fellers who killed pappy had only been hired to fight. When I shot the first of them, the other two lit out. Joe'd heard about pappy and come down to even things up. So he insisted on riding with me after the other pair. We trailed them down to Trinity. Just outside town, we found a sharecropper's wife in labor and Joe made me stop to help her. It took time and while I worked at it, he went into Trinity. Seems the two jaspers knew I was after them and were waiting in a saloon ready to kill me as soon as I walked in."

"Only Joe Brambile got there first," Dusty said as Doc paused.

"Sure. They didn't know he was siding me. So he walked in there, picked a fight with them and killed them both. If I'd been alone— Well, I wouldn't be sat here talking like it's going out of fashion."

"I'll have Waco cover the game tonight," Dusty said.

"That's not the answer, and you know it," Doc replied. "Everybody's just waiting to see how I handle it. Who'll believe anything the boy says?"

"There're few who'd call him a liar—and none twice."

"They'd not call him it to his face, but the thoughts'd be there. Don't forget that nobody but us bunch knows just how good he is."

During the time when he was learning peace officer work in Mulrooney, Waco's instructions had included the detection of crooked gambling moves and gear. Taught by an honest gambler, who knew such things to protect his interests, Waco possessed a knowledge equal to Doc's.

"That's as right as the off side of a horse," Dusty admitted.

"And you don't want it knowing just yet," Doc went on.

Even in Mulrooney Waco's talents went unnoticed. So Dusty planned to use the youngster as an unsuspected observer, relying on the dishonest gamblers in town counting Doc as the only one they needed to watch.

"It'd be easier if nobody knew," Dusty said. "But—"

"I took the oath along with the badge, Dusty, like I warned Joe. Now I'll stake my life that he's on the level, but I'm going to be there when the game starts and make sure he is."

"And when we've proved it, we'll ram the lie straight

down the throats of whoever started it," Dusty promised.

Standing at the forefront of the crowd gathered around the table set up for the big game, Doc Leroy watched a fine demonstration of how stud poker should be played. All the players, Brambile, two cattle-buyers, a trail boss and a buffalo hunter appeared capable of holding their own in any company.

Any remaining doubts the Texans might have felt died when Jordan sent to the office requesting Doc's presence to supervise the game. The saloonkeeper insisted that he wanted protection, as such a high-stake game might be the cause of the "readers" being smuggled into his establishment. Dusty and the others knew that aspect of the affair to be a lie. Before the night was out, Doc's reputation would be cleared, or broken. Already the careful campaign of rumor-spreading had done its insidious work. Even people disposed to favor the Texans were wondering if there could be any truth in what they heard.

"After all," was the question being asked, "how did that slim Texan learn so much about card-cheating?"

So, although a high-stake game could be expected to attract kibitzers, a larger than usual crowd had assembled. Some of them, Doc guessed, had never watched card-players before and cared little for the subtleties of the play. Much interest manifested itself when Jordan insisted on Doc examining the deck to be used. Holding down a desire to wipe away the saloonkeeper's smirk with the barrel of his Colt, Doc complied. He found, as he knew he would, the deck to be a twin to the "readers" confiscated that morning.

Within the space of one pot Doc knew that his presence would not normally have been required. Every man in the game clearly played high-stake poker often enough to be well aware of its dangers and could be relied upon to detect "readers" or other cheating methods.

Standing at Brambile's right side, Doc commanded a

clear view of the whole table. He could see no hint that any of the players intended to try improving on the dictates of luck. In that class of company, the use of "shiners"—small mirror-like objects placed so as to reflect the face of a card as it was dealt—would be located without the need for outside help. Any players trying to use the "shark's grip" while dealing stood a better than fair chance of being asked to desist, or quit the game. When dealing, each man kept the cards low to the table top and without the pauses necessary to allow cover for the various methods of peeking at the top of the deck.

Hand after hand passed, played with tense appreciation for the finer points of mathematical chances and bluff. Doc found watching the play particularly enjoyable. Here was no cowhand game, with laughter and conversation going on continuously while each player stuck in to the bitter end, hoping for a last card miracle even when one would be an impossibility. A hand showing no signs of improvement potential went into the dead-wood and its receiver sat back silently until the completion of the pot. While the betting rose gradually higher, no player won so consistently as to arouse suspicion. Doc began to wonder if Dusty had overestimated the danger.

When a worried-looking Mousey had been brought into the office, he confirmed that he had picked up the story from an employee at the Blazing Pine. However nothing conclusive arose, for the others could not learn where various citizens had heard their version of the rumor.

Taking up the cards, Joe Brambile sat riffle-stacking them with the casually thorough way of the professional gambler. A movement of the crowd drew Doc's attention to where a waiter was approaching the table carrying a tray of refreshments for the players. At the same moment Doc became aware that Jordan had come up and was standing to his left. Halting, the waiter allowed the deck to be cut by the trail boss. Then he moved forward, holding the tray out in Brambile's direction. Surprise and irritation showed on the gambler's face.

Cold apprehension bit into Doc as he realized the moment had come. From under the edge of the tray showed just a faint, but very significant hint of alien color. Stepping forward, Doc knocked the tray out of the man's hands. Doing so brought into view the deck of cards, with identical backs to those in play, previously held concealed beneath it.

"I never thought you'd try ringing in a cold deck, Joe," Doc said as the waiter let the cards fall to the table and backed hurriedly away to be halted by the press of the crowd.

Immediately silence fell on the room and the kibitzers drew back. Such an accusation normally heralded the crackle of shots. Of all the players, only Brambile appeared unmoved.

"Now that pains me, boy," the gambler said. "Not so much for myself, although I thought you'd trust me, but for these gentlemen who've done me the honor of such a noble game. Do you sell them so short that you reckon I'd think to get away with such a hoary wheeze as that?"

A neat compliment and it did a little to lessen the cold suspicion that showed on the other players' faces. Seeing the indecision, Jordan moved forward. He had hoped that Doc might ignore the deliberately exposed cards. In which case the waiter was to drop them on the table, apparently fumbling the hand over. When the scheme started to go wrong, Jordan advanced to correct it.

"Well, I'm damned!" he said, speaking hastily, in what he figured to be the most damning way possible. "You took all the decks of 'readers' that somebody tricked me into buying, deputy."

"So?" Doc asked.

"So how come your card-shark friend's brought one here?"

"You've got real good eyes, *hombre,*" Doc said quietly, but his words carried as well as the saloonkeeper's blustering tones. "Damned good if you can see they're marked cards from where you're stood."

Suddenly Jordan realized his mistake. Seeing that the crowd followed Doc's meaning, he lost his head. Not entirely, however, for he had taken precautions when setting up the trap. Doc faced Jordan, tense and ready, but behind him stood Tatem. Instead of grabbing at his gun, certain to cause a hurried scattering of the kibitzers around him and warn Doc of the danger, Tatem eased it stealthily out of the holster. So carefully did he move that Doc remained unaware of the peril.

If Doc failed to see Tatem, the same did not apply to Brambile.

Sending his chair skidding backwards, the gambler left it at a speed a much younger man might have envied. He crashed into Doc, knocking the deputy aside just as Tatem brought up the gun and fired. Instead of driving into Doc's back, the bullet carved a gash through Brambile's shoulder. Fortunately it flew on without striking any of the room's occupants and ended its flight harmlessly in the wall.

Showing that speed and understanding of the situation seemingly born into Western crowds, the kibitzers recognized danger and dived for shelter. Still staggering from Brambile's thrust, Doc twisted to meet the threat from behind. His almost boneless-looking right hand made a sight-defying flicker, drawing the ivory-handled Colt so fast that gun and hand appeared to connect together in midair. Even as Tatem prepared to fire again, Doc shot him in the head. Doing so caused Doc to turn his back on Jordan. Snarling in fury, the saloonkeeper began to jerk the Colt from his waistband. The batwing doors burst open and Mark Counter lunged through from where he had been watching the proceedings.

"Jordan!" the blond giant roared, right hand dipping and bringing up the off side Colt in the smooth, effortless appearing, yet lightning fast manner that set the expert apart from the merely good.

Flame flashed from the seven and a half inch barrel of Mark's Colt. The bullet slammed into Jordan's ribs while the saloonkeeper still vacillated between killing Doc and facing the new threat. Jerking under the impact, Jordan retained his hold on his gun and tried to turn it. Without a moment of hesitation Mark acted in the manner of a trained peace officer. Wounded or not, as long as Jordan held the gun he menaced lives. In his hurt condition, even while trying to down his assailant, he might start shooting wild. So Mark thumb-cocked the Colt on its recoil and fired again. The bullet drove into Jordan's skull and tumbled him in a limp pile to the floor.

The waiter who had delivered the tray-hidden cards rose from behind a table and tried to escape. Racing across the room, he tore open a side door and started through it. Almost immediately he returned, walking backwards with the barrel of the Kid's rifle poking into his throat.

"You surely ain't figuring on leaving yet a-whiles, are you?" drawled the Kid, keeping the man moving backwards with insistent prods in the adam's apple. "Why for shame, the fun's just starting."

At the same moment Waco crashed in through the other side door, ready, willing and most eager to deal with any fuss from the rest of the saloon staff. Much to his annoyance, Jordan's employees showed a remarkable lack of loyalty and none offered even a token objection to his demise. Maybe if the saloonkeeper had been alive to hand out rewards, things would not have gone so quietly. Backing a dead man paid off in nothing but grief.

"You hit, Doc?" Mark asked worriedly, advancing with gun in hand.

"Not me," Doc replied, holstering his Colt and leaping to the gambler's side. "Joe saved me."

Leaving Doc to care for Brambile, Mark turned to the

busines of tidying up. Faced by the blond giant, the Kid, who no longer looked young or innocent, and Waco, the waiter decided that honesty was the best policy.

"Jordan told me to bring the cards!" he yelped. "I told him a fool game like it'd never work, but he said I had to do it."

"Pick those cards up real careful, Gil," Mark said to the trail boss. "See if you can get them up as they were when he dropped them."

"I should be able to," the trail boss answered, guessing what Mark had in mind and willing to help.

The task did not prove difficult. When the waiter let the cards fall, they bounced on the table and slid apart. However by shoving them back carefully, Gil managed to return them to their original positions.

"Some of you town gents come around," Mark ordered. "Gil, take Joe's place and deal out six stud hands."

Eagerly several citizens moved forward, the railroad depot's yard-master and his storekeeper companion among the first to volunteer their services. All of the men watched as Gil began to deal the cards as if for a normal game. Mark felt a touch of apprehension as the pasteboard flipped on to the table. If Jordan had foreseen the contingency, people might still need convincing of Brambile and Doc's innocence.

Before the second round of cards had been dealt, Mark began to relax. The idea of a cold deck—specially arranged before the game—was to entice the others players into betting, while ensuring that the dealer held the winning hand. Under no circumstances would the cards exposed by Gil's dealing do so with such skilled players. However the blond giant kept quiet, letting the deal continue but watching the crowd's faces. Soon he saw that they too realized that Joe Brambile could not win on the cards dealt from the deck.

"And he sure as hell wouldn't want to chance ringing in

another one later," commented the buffalo hunter.

"Well, deputy," Dinger Magee, the yard-master said. "Looks like there's been a whole heap of lying done today about you."

"But you sure showed them for what they was," the storekeeper, Oliver Titmuss, went on. "That's no cold deck, so I'd say they was just trying to make you look bad."

"As long as you folks're satisfied—" Mark put in, looking around the room and waiting for a rumble of agreement to end. "All right, this place's closed until we learn who Jordan's heirs might be."

Nobody objected and soon only the deputies remained to watch the saloon's staff carry out the order.

Dusty was sitting in the office reading a telegraph message from Lieutenant Ed Ballinger when a jubilant Waco brought the news. Although Ballinger had failed to learn who purchased the shotgun used by Jackley, Dusty did not feel disappointed. No matter that the man behind the murder attempt remained unidentified, Dusty knew that he and the floating outfit had won an important battle that night. Their position in Trail End was strengthened by Doc's sense of duty over-riding loyalty to an old friend.

PART THREE

Bellamy's Try

Stepping from his office, Evan Bellamy swept a glance around the room as if searching for somebody. He hardly gave the faro table any attention until forced to by a considerable row which rose from around it. Laughter, whoops and cattle-calls rang out, then one of the players, a cowhand, spoke in a ringing voice.

"Yahoo! Just look-it that! I just knowed that lil ole four of spades'd be riding drag on the king of diamond's trail herd."

A slight frown creased the saloonkeeper's face as he watched the game's dealer, with a sour expression, shove a stack of chips across to swell the heap already piled before the speaker. Looking no less sour, the floor manager joined his boss at the office door. Big, heavily-built, florid-faced, Flint Pascoe wore gambler's dress and carried a low-hanging gun. Floor managers were rarely selected for gentle nature or peaceable dispositions; but even in a town such as Trail End recently used to be, Pascoe stood alone for his treatment of customers who offended the house's ideas of good behavior.

"That damned beef-head's doing real well, boss," Pascoe said in his normal growling tones. "He come in with maybe ten dollars and's run it up. Been betting winners, losers, every which damned way and they've come out of that box like he plucked 'em special. Now he's just called the turn and got all three of 'em right."

Calling the turn, betting that one could guess the order in which the last three cards from the box would be dealt, paid off at odds of four to one. As the cowhand wagered correctly that the seven of clubs would lead the way, followed by the king of diamonds, with the four of spades bringing up the rear like a drag-rider on a trail herd, he had reason to sound happy.

"How much's he won?" Bellamy demanded.

"Close to eight hundred. Like I said, he's been betting high, wide and lucky. There's nothing we can do to stop him, way his luck's going."

Which point Bellamy did not require explaining. Five days ago, before the coming of Dusty Fog, such a state of affairs could never have happened; or if, by some miracle, it did, the answer would be easy enough to find. In only five short days the condition of the town had so deteriorated that a winning gambler could not be cheated, or slipped a drugged drink at the bar then relieved of his ill-gotten gains.

For a moment Bellamy stood glaring at the faro layout and thinking of ordering the dealer to try something. However cheating at faro called for a special type of dealing box. Bellamy possessed such a box, but recalled the unpleasant habit of making unexpected visits practiced by Dusty Fog and the deputies. No doubt Doc Leroy had taught his companions what to look for and they could recognize the distinctive shape of a brace box. Knowing the penalty for cheating to be the closing of the place involved, Bellamy did not dare risk passing the order.

Yet there might be other ways to relieve the cowhand of

his winnings. Catching the dealer's eye, Bellamy made a sign.

"That's it, fellers," the dealer announced, turning the card box on to its side. "This gent's bust the bank."

"And it couldn't've happened to a nicer feller," grinned the cowhand, scooping up the money the look-out exchanged for his chips. Then he shoved twenty dollars across the table to the dealer. "Here, friend. Come on, boys, belly up to the bar on me."

"Where's Laura?" Bellamy asked Pascoe, selecting the prettiest of his female employees for the work ahead.

"Upstairs with that cattle-buyer. We can't disturb him."

"Damn it. Get one of the oth—"

Before Bellamy could finish, the cowhand's voice came to him. "You boys stop on here and drink this up. I'm going to Annie's place to see that gal I was with last night."

"She was sure something, Frank boy," grinned another of the trail crew, accepting a fist full of money from his friend.

"You're telling *me?"* grinned the winner, rolling his eyes ecstatically at the thought. "Now there's a gal I'd take home to meet my mother—only I couldn't trust pappy."

Followed by laughter, cheers and bawdy suggestions from his friends, the cowhand started across the room. Letting out a low growl, Pascoe made as if to follow but Bellamy caught his arm.

"Let him go. It's safer this way. Go get Baines and Croft for me."

"Sure, boss," Pascoe answered, turning and crashing into a small man who came towards them. "Damn you, Mousey, get from underfoot."

"I'm sorry, Mr. Pascoe," Mousey answered mildly and scuttled nervously by.

Halting at a blackjack table, Mousey watched Pascoe approach two men and speak. Following the pair with his eyes, the little informer drew certain conclusions which he felt might prove profitable. So he turned on his heel and left the saloon in search of a customer for his findings.

When he had led the two men into the privacy of his office, Bellamy wasted no time. Both the tall, gangling Croft and shorter, rubbery Baines guessed at why they were summoned and showed no surprise at the orders they received.

"Get after that cowpoke," Bellamy snapped. "He's going to Annie's house."

"We can find him easy enough," grinned Croft.

"Don't kill him if there's any other way!" the saloonkeeper barked.

Humane or moral considerations did not cause the order, it arose from caution. Every instinct Bellamy possessed warned him that Dusty Fog would not rest until the cowhand's murderers were brought in. While the robbery would be investigated, there would not be the same relentless determination as there would if the cowhand should be killed.

Needing no further instructions, Croft and Baines left by the rear door. Despite the fact that he left before them, the cowhand did not know the town so well as the men and they beat him to his destination. In the interests of avoiding the wrong kind of attention, the brothel run by Annie Gash stood in the center of a small clump of trees. Selecting a place half way through the clump, Croft and Baine hid behind a tree on each side of the path. They had not been in position for a minute when the sound of a cowhand song reached their ears. Through the gloom of the trees they saw their victim walking uncertainly towards them.

Having handled similar chores, the two men knew what to do. They waited until the cowhand came level, then Croft stepped out to wrap long, wiry arms about him. Before he could struggle, Baines knocked off his Stetson. Up and down with smooth, practiced precision rose the rubbery man's other hand. The leather-wrapped, lead-loaded billy struck the cowhand's skull and he went limp in Croft's grasp.

"Neat, Bainesy," Croft grinned, allowing the unconscious cowhand to slip to the ground. "You're sure handy with that sap."

"I ain't been getting much practice these last few days," Baines answered, kneeling alongside the cowhand and rifling his pockets deftly. "And I ain't felt this kind of money in months."

"There's some'd say it's a pity we have to hand it to Bellamy," Croft remarked. "Us taking all the chances to get it and all."

"You wouldn't be hinting we kept it for ourselves, now would you?" Baines asked. "That'd be dishonest."

"Sure would. Only this here town's getting all played out and a couple of talented gents like us could easy find work some other place—if we had the train fare to get there."

"Which we ain't. Way them Texans' been acting, a fellow don't know where his next meal's coming from."

"*That* won't worry you pair for a spell."

The unexpected voice from behind them jolted Croft and Baines out of their complacent reverie. While it did not carry the accents of any of their fellow workers sent along to prevent the course they were discussing, the voice meant somebody had witnessed their crime. Unless they missed their guess, the witness hailed from the Lone Star State; the drawl in his voice told them that. Suddenly they became aware that being on their knees alongside the unconscious body of their victim was far from an ideal situation in which to find themselves.

Twisting around as they started to rise, Croft and Baines stared through the gloomy darkness of the path. Despite the lack of light, they recognized the figure before them. Those black clothes, with the badge glinting on the shirt, must belong to the Ysabel Kid.

"Get h—!" Baines began.

A laudable ambition which might have reached fulfillment had it not been for the Kid's reluctance to be "got".

Advancing fast on his moccasin-clad feet, he swung the rifle in a smooth arc. Caught under the jaw with the butt, Croft pitched backwards and sprawled across their victim.

Hands full of their loot, Baines found himself at even a greater disadvantage than the unencumbered Croft. While he tried to decide whether to pocket the money or drop it, the decision was taken from his hands. Coming down from striking Croft, the Winchester's brass butt plate smashed into the side of Baines' jaw. Even as bright lights seemed to explode all around Baines, he heard feet running along the path. Then everything went black and he landed on the ground, temporarily losing all interest in the affair.

"Damn it, Lon!" protested Waco, coming to a halt, and glaring at his companion. "You've done it all. You're getting a regular hawg, way you take on."

"Don't you worry none, boy," the Kid answered. "I'll save one for you the next time. Ole Mousey sure called it right."

Having seen Croft and Baines enter Bellamy's office and adding it to the various other happenings at the First Chance, Mousey guessed that an attempt would be made to relieve the cowhand of his winnings. So he sought out Dusty Fog to sell his knowledge. Meeting the Ysabel Kid and Waco making their rounds, he gave them the details and requested that his part in preventing the crime be reported to the marshal.

"He's been hit hard, Lon," Waco commented, having rolled Croft ungently aside and knelt to examine the victim. "We'd best get him on to a bed."

"Go tell Annie to have him took inside," the Kid answered and drew a pair of handcuffs from where they had been hanging to his gunbelt. "I'll tend to this pair."

Going to the house, Waco stepped into the parlor. Small, petite, looking like anything but the madam of a brothel, Annie Gash walked up to the deputy. In a long experience around hog-ranches she had never come across men like the Texans brought in by the Governor to tame Trail End. Most honest peace officers, especially when employed on such a task, would have closed the brothels. So when Dusty Fog visited her on the day after his arrival, Annie expected an order to get out of town. Her next thought, when the order failed to come, was how much staying open would cost. To her amazement she found that Dusty intended to leave the houses open, without payment of bribes. All he asked was that they provided a service to visitors, but refrained from practices such as robbery.

So when she heard of Baines and Croft's actions on the path, she hurried to state her innocence. Cursing the two men, she readily agreed to bring in their victim and bed him down with every comfort. An uneasy feeling bit at her as Waco showed no inclination to follow the bouncers outside.

"Cap'n Fog's not going to be happy at this, ma'am," the youngster said.

"But you won't tell him—" Annie said, reaching towards the décolleté top of her dress and the purse which swung inside it.

"He'll have to know, ma'am," Waco interrupted. "Could be he'll reckon you get a cut from those fellers."

"The hell I do!" she hissed.

"Who's the boss since Burger got shot, ma'am?" Waco asked.

"Boss?"

"Dusty's going to start wondering how many more fellers'll get their heads whomped coming here. Might even figure the place's not safe to keep open."

"How old are you?" Annie asked, just a touch of admiration flickering on her face.

"Old enough to be wearing a badge—again."

"You had good teachers."

"The best, ma'am," Waco assured her. "You were saying who the boss is now."

"Look, deputy," Annie said earnestly. "I don't know— You have to believe me. After A—Burger died, that slimy clerk who works for Grosvenor came along and told me I'd got to start paying the take to him."

"And you agreed?"

"He'd got some tough backing, Tatem from the Blazing Pine, Flint Pascoe, the Kraut, Attick from Coulton's place. That kind of company I don't tangle with. So I paid the take over. You won't let on that I told you?"

"Only to Cap'n Fog," Waco promised. "And you can trust him to keep quiet. Say, wasn't there anybody from Eggars' place along?"

"Not that I saw," the madam answered and looked to where her bouncers were carrying the cowhand inside. "Take him up to Dolly's room, boys."

"I'll send the doctor, ma'am," Waco said.

A faint grin creased Annie's face. "There's no need for that," she said.

"You mean he's here?"

"Why not? This's the best house in town, my gals're clean. Why shouldn't he be here?"

"Seeing's he's a bachelor, I can't think of a reason," Waco admitted with a grin back.

"Say, if you're ever feeling like—"

"I'll keep it in mind."

"You can have the pick of the house, handsome," Annie promised. "And I wish I was young enough to be it."

"Why you don't look a day over twenty-one, ma'am," Waco complimented and walked out of the room.

Pascoe, the late Tatem, May's head bouncer the Kraut, Attick, floor manager of the Good Fortune. Top hands from four of the leading places of entertainment in town. Most likely Dusty would find the information useful, especially as Mousey had failed to learn who had assumed control of the brothels. However, there was another matter needing more immediate attention.

"I thought you'd gone up for your pleasure, boy," the Kid remarked as Waco returned from the house.

"Yah! It's better'n stealing hosses to give to the gal's

pappy like you Injuns," the youngster answered. "They said much?"

"Not a sight. Let's take 'em back to the office."

Hauling the handcuffed pair to their feet, Waco gave them the order to start walking.

"I'll say one thing, Lon," the young deputy commented as their prisoners obeyed. "It sure come as a surprise when Bellamy let us know about this pair."

"Just goes to show how wrong you can be about a feller," the Kid answered, apparently unaware of the interest the words aroused in Croft and Baines. "All along I've been thinking Bellamy was bad, but he surely acted like a public-spirited citizen when he saw these *hombres* follow the cowhand out of his place."

"Smart, too," Waco drawled, watching the effect of the words on their prisoners. "Figured they aimed to sneak up and steal that cowhand's winnings."

Baines' breath came in snorting grunts, while Croft, linked to his companion by the handcuffs, darted glances back at the deputies.

"He only called it wrong on one thing though, Lon," the youngster continued after a pause to allow the meaning of the words to sink in. "You didn't have to kill 'em."

"Maybe they're not a couple of real desperate owlhoots with rewards on their hides," drawled the Kid. "Tell you though, Waco, I near on did what Bellamy said, shot 'em first and told 'em to quit robbing that lil Texas boy after."

Letting out curses, Baines and Croft tried to turn. Their manacled wrists halted the attempt and slammed them back to back. However that did not prevent two wrath-filled faces turning towards the deputies.

"Did Bellamy tell you that?" Croft demanded.

"Now how else do you figure we come on you just right?" asked the Kid. "I tell you, Waco, Cap'n Fog's going to look a whole heap friendlier on Mr. Bellamy after this."

Put that way, the words dispelled any lingering doubts the two prisoners felt. Ever since recovering enough to think, each man had attributed their capture to no more than bad luck. Guessing what lay on their prisoners' minds, Waco started the conversation and the Kid went along with it. Their purpose was to arouse suspicion and they succeeded very well.

Knowing nothing of Mousey's actions, Croft and Baines saw no reason to doubt what they heard. Only Bellamy knew for sure that they had gone to rob the cowhand, although probably Pascoe suspected it. Nor did the furious pair need to look far to find a motive for their employer's treachery. Conditions in Trail End were growing gradually worse, from the point of the dishonest citizens, and the closing of the Blazing Pine allowed the marshal more time to concentrate on the other places.

Wishing to improve his standing with Dusty Fog, Bellamy had decided to sacrifice two of his men as a gesture of his public-spirited nature. If anything the myth that he had suggested killing them both on sight added strength to the credibility of the story; dead men being notorious for their silence and not talking out of turn.

"Damn it!" Croft wailed, almost tugging Baines' arm out of its socket in his desire to turn and vent his righteous indignation. "It was Bellamy who sent us after that feller."

"G'wan!" answered the Kid. "You're just saying that out of ornery meanness."

"It's the living truth!" Baines protested, struggling around to face the deputies. "Go get Pascoe, the floor manager, he told us that Bellamy wanted to see us in the office."

"He'll tell you that," Croft agreed, but with a complete lack of confidence in his voice.

"Oh, sure!" agreed Waco. "I can just see Mr. Bellamy fetching you into his office and telling you to rob that feller—in front of a witness."

The more the Texans appeared to refuse to accept the story, the more insistent Croft and Baines became. By the time the prisoners reached the marshal's office, their fury had reached such a pitch over the "betrayal" that they willingly told everything. In the presence of witnesses collected from the street by Waco, Baines and Croft saw their statements written down, read out to the witnesses and fixed their signatures on the paper.

"What now, Dusty?" asked the Kid after lodging the prisoners in separate cells and returning to the office.

"Let's go see what Mr. Bellamy has to say," the small Texan replied.

"How do we go?" said Mark, putting the question on all the deputies' minds.

"The right way," Dusty answered and nodded towards the rack of weapons on the wall.

One of Mousey's traits had always been a tendency to run with the fox and hunt alongside the hounds. After seeing the deputies start off after Baines and Croft, the little informer made his way to the marshal's office. Instead of entering to collect payment for his services, he went through the alley by the building and found a place close by from where he could keep unseen watch on the rear door.

Just as he figured, the deputies brought their captives that way, avoiding the main street so as to prevent word reaching Bellamy of the arrest. From scraps of conversation that reached his ears, Mousey concluded that Baines and Croft intended to take their employer with them into jail. Still he waited, wanting certain proof before going about his business. He read significance in the way the Kid took the prisoners into the building, while Waco went around it and on to the street. By the time Mousey arrived, the youngster was already walking towards the front door accompanied by two townsmen. Again the little informer waited a short time, then he walked along in front of the building and looked through its window. Seeing Dusty writing while Croft talked, Mousey knew what had happened and saw the way to pick up more money.

Turning, the little man hurried to the First Chance Saloon. He entered and saw Bellamy standing at the bar.

Crossing the room, Mousey halted at the saloonkeeper's side. Bellamy ignored him and continued to look at the front door as if expecting a visitor.

"You've got trouble, Mr. Bellamy," Mousey muttered out of the corner of his mouth. "Real bad trouble."

Slowly Bellamy turned and looked the little man up and down. "What kind of trouble'd that be?"

"With the marshal."

Coming along the counter to serve Mousey, the bartender saw his employer's head-shake and withdrew to attend to other customers. Swinging to face the bar, Bellamy appeared to ignore the little man. However both of them looked into the bar mirror. Watching Mousey's reflection, Bellamy took out his wallet and eased a five dollar bill into view. Another bill followed as the saloonkeeper saw no response from the man at his side; a third as Mousey still failed to show any sign of acceptance. For a moment Bellamy hesitated, then his lips drew into a tight line and he added a fourth bill. Knowing just how far he dare push the affair, Mousey nodded his head.

"This's a whole heap of money," Bellamy growled. "You'd best earn it."

"Those two boys you sent after the drunken cowhand, Mr. Bellamy—" Mousey answered.

"What about them?"

"They won't be coming back. The Ysabel Kid and that young feller, Waco, done caught 'em right in the act."

"How'd you know about all this?"

"I'd been down to Annie's place," Mousey answered, having expected the question and thought up an explanation. "Heard this feller coming. He sounded all liquored up, so I hid. Figured there might be a chance to roll him. Only your boys licked me to it."

"My boys?" Bellamy spat, but did not replace the money.

"They talked enough to let me—and them deputies—know."

"Those stupid—!" Bellamy began, then he slid the payment along the bar. "You want to earn another ten?"

"As long as it's nothing dangerous," Mousey agreed.

"It's—" Bellamy started, then looked across the room to where a man had entered. "Just go over and feed your face, I'll send word when I need you."

"Sure thing," Mousey answered, swinging away without apparently noticing that the newcomer was walking straight to where Bellamy stood waiting.

However the little informer studied the man while going to the free-lunch counter and helping himself. Tall, lean unshaven, with straggly hair showing from under a Stetson decorated by an eagle feather thrust into its band, the man's face struck no responsive chord in Mousey's memory. However his dress told a story to eyes which knew the signs. Fringed buckskin shirt, filthy old cavalry trousers, Sioux moccasins, with a wampum belt that carried a brace of 1860 Army Colts in cavalry draw holsters. Not a cowhand and, judging by the Union blue color of the pants, unlikely to be a trail-drive scout. A cavalry scout, maybe; or another profession sprang to mind. Without allowing his interest to become noticeable, Mousey stared again at the man's legs. The material of the pants showed a stiffness beyond ordinary dirt and suggested an answer; which in turn presented another problem.

"What in hell'd Bellamy want with a buffalo hunter right now?" the informer mused. "I'd've thought he'd be headed out of town as fast as his hoss could run."

Yet instead of taking that basic precaution, Bellamy led the newcomer into his office. Mousey swung his head hurriedly back towards the food as Pascoe called a bouncer to him and pointed in the informer's direction. Then, as Pascoe followed his boss, the bouncer slouched over to Mousey's side.

"You gotta stay put for a spell, Mousey," the big man ordered. "Boss says for me to see you does."

Stuffing half a hard-boiled egg into his mouth, Mousey nodded. "Sure, if that's what he wants."

Then the little man gave thought to Bellamy's visitor. No amount of ordinary business could have held the saloonkeeper after the news Mousey had delivered. In fact Mousey could think of no business Bellamy might have with a buffalo hunter. At one time Trail End had drawn a fair proportion of its income from such men, but not recently. Already the relentless slaughter had reduced the once vast herds to a mere dribble in Kansas. So the easy money that could be picked up meat- or hide-hunting dried off. Where once a man owning a rifle could leave town and return in a month with his wagon creaking under the weight of meat or flints,* the sight of a buffalo became rare and its hunters fell on lean times.

It seemed unlikely that Bellamy, even without the threat of arrest hovering over his head, would consider investing in a buffalo hunt.

Although Mousey felt that Dusty Fog might be interested in the meeting, he saw no immediate way of carrying the news. Clearly the bouncer intended to stick at his side and ensure that he waited until Bellamy needed him. While wondering how he might escape, without arousing suspicions, he saw Pascoe leave the office and come towards him.

"You know where Lawyer Grosvenor lives, Mousey?" the floor manager growled.

"Sure."

"Boss says for you to take him this letter, and to get there with it real fast," Pascoe said, holding out a sealed envelope with a five dollar bill on top.

"I'll see to it," Mousey promised, slipping both items into his pocket.

"Another thing," Pascoe said, catching the little man's arm. "Look at the time. If the lawyer says it took you more than five minutes to reach him, I'll make you wish your mammy and pappy never even met the once."

* Flints: trade name for buffalo skins.

"You can trust me," the little man whined.

"I'd better never have cause not to," growled Pascoe. "Get going."

Freed from the grip, Mousey hurried out of the barroom. A man engaged in his line of work lived on a razor-edge. To succeed, stay alive and healthy, he must know the chances he could safely take. Even if the law arrested Bellamy, his men would be at liberty. So Mousey must do the work he received payment for, or take the consequences. Knowing what the consequences would be, he decided to deliver the letter first and then take word to Dusty about the saloon-keeper's visitor.

Five minutes after Mousey left the First Chance, its bat-wing doors swung open and two members of the civic law enforcement body entered. At first the arrival of Dusty Fog and Mark Counter attracted no attention among the customers. Already folk around Trail End had grown used to seeing pairs of lawmen making the rounds, or paying unexpected visits to the saloons. Yet slowly a growing feeling rose that this might not be an ordinary, routine visit.

Silence dropped on the room as man after man's eyes went to the two Texans, paying especial attention to the weapon in Mark Counter's big hands. While some Kansas lawmen made a habit of carrying a double-barrel shotgun at all times, that had never been the way of Dusty and his deputies. Only when expecting trouble, or going into what they expected to develop to a fight, did the Texans take the ten-gauge pacifiers from the wall rack. That they had entered the saloon with Mark carrying one struck most people present as highly significant.

Looking around, Dusty guessed that word of the arrests had reached Bellamy. He noticed that three bartenders were standing behind the bar instead of the usual one, while various other saloon employees had gathered in strategic positions around the room.

"You wanting something?" demanded the house manager, coming forward and halting before the Texans.

"Where's your boss?" Dusty asked.

"Why?"

"If you'd do, I wouldn't waste time asking for him. Is he in the office?"

"Maybe."

"We'll just go take a look," Dusty stated.

"You got a warrant?" Pascoe demanded.

"This do?" Dusty asked, left hand crossing his body.

Half a second later Pascoe looked into the barrel of the Colt from the small Texan's right side holster, its cocking click sounding inordinately loud in his ears.

At the same moment several things happened to damp down any desire the other saloon workers might have wished to express an opinion on the matter.

Mark swung the shotgun which had trailed from his left hand, slapping its barrels into his right palm and thumbing back the hammers. Casual though the move appeared, it ended with the men hovering behind Pascoe facing the twin, gaping muzzles of the gun. Immediately they forgot their intentions of objecting to the intrusion of their employer's privacy.

Shoving open the left side door, Waco entered and his shotgun moved in a leisurely arc that froze any opposition on his side of the room. On the other flank, Doc's appearance brought peace and tranquility where there might have been discord. Finally the Kid's arrival from the rear prevented intervention by the bartenders. Instead of carrying a shotgun, he placed his peace-keeping reliance on his rifle; but nobody thought the less of him for that.

"You heard the marshal, *hombre,*" Mark said. "Is that warrant enough for you?"

"Yeah," the floor manager muttered sullenly.

Any doubts Pascoe might have held about Dusty's speed on the draw had died on receiving such a practical demonstration. While he realized that answer lowered his standing around the saloon, he could do nothing but give it. Nor did he offer to make a move as the Texans walked by him. While Dusty Fog and Mark Counter no longer faced him, their friends stood ideally placed to prevent any attempt at avenging the loss of face.

On reaching the door of the private office, Mark swung his shotgun into what bayonet-fighters termed the "high port" position. Bracing himself, he delivered a kick intended to spring the lock. From the way the door shook but held, he concluded it had bolts fitted as added security.

"I'll have to do it the hard way," the blond giant remarked, handing his shotgun to Dusty.

Dropping his shoulder, Mark hurled himself forward. One hundred and ninety pounds of solid bone and muscle struck home with an impact that made the whole wall shake. Wood cracked and metal shrieked as screws tore from their hold in the door. Then the whole door itself burst inwards and Mark disappeared into the office, followed an instant later by Dusty.

The small Texan lit down in Bellamy's room ready to use the shotgun, but the need did not arise. Apart from Mark, standing on the ruined door, Dusty had the office to himself. Looking around he noticed the safe's door standing open, the shelves inside bare. While the room's other door also had bolts fitted, they were not fastened. That told how Bellamy left the building.

"He's run out," Mark said unnecessarily. "Somebody must've warned him."

"Mousey, likely," Dusty replied. "I thought I saw him looking in the window while I was taking down those two owlhoots' statements."

"If you'd've said, I could have gone out and caught him."

"Why?"

"To hold him in the pokey so's he couldn't warn Bellamy."

"And stop ole Mousey picking up a little eating money?"

Dusty drawled. "For shame, Mark, I never thought you'd show such a mean streak."

"But Bellamy's run—" Mark began.

"Which's not what I'd expect from an honest man," Dusty interrupted. "And I'll bet there's plenty in town who feel the same way."

Swinging abruptly towards Dusty, the blond giant towered over him with an expression that brought a grin to his face.

"Damn it all, Dusty!" Mark spluttered. "You figured on this happening."

"Let's just say that, knowing Mousey, I hoped it would," Dusty replied. "We didn't have a real strong case with just those two's word."

"Maybe not," Mark admitted. "There's no chance of picking up his trail in the dark, though."

"He'll keep—and if he doesn't come back I'll be satisfied," Dusty answered. "Let's go tell them to close up."

"So you didn't see the boss," Pascoe said, coming forward as Dusty and Mark left the office.

"Nope," admitted Dusty, noticing that the man had removed and let fall his gunbelt while they were out of the room.

"Maybe he's gone to see his kin-folks," Pascoe sneered and the other saloon workers bellowed out their approval of his wit.

"Could be," Dusty drawled. "Only I don't know what's pleasuring you bunch."

"Huh?" grunted the puzzled floor manager and the laughter died uncertainly off to nothing.

"You're all out of work. This place's closed from now."

"Yeah?" snarled Pascoe menacingly. "Suppose I tell you to go to hell?"

"Jackley tried," Dusty replied.

"Maybe I'm tougher than he was," Pascoe snarled. "If you didn't have that scatter, I'd—"

"Here, Mark," Dusty put in, tossing the gun to the blond giant.

The moment Dusty's eyes left him, Pascoe lunged forward. Big hands reached out, to close on air. Sidestepping the moment the shotgun left his hands, Dusty evaded the attack. Then, as Pascoe's rush carried him forward, Dusty snapped a vicious kick straight to his groin. Pain almost too unbearable to be imagined ripped into the big man. Letting out a hoarse screech of pain, he clutched at the injured area and doubled over. Dusty turned, bounding after the man and caught him by pants seat and jacket collar. With a surging heave, Dusty hurled Pascoe across the room. Unable to stop himself, propelled by a strength out of all proportion to the small frame which applied it, the floor manager crashed head first into the wall. Arriving with a force almost equaling Mark's charge against the door, although the point of impact differed, Pascoe collapsed. Only the fact that he wore a Stetson saved him from worse injury; although prying it loose from over his eyes later caused him considerable pain.

"No, mister," Dusty said, despite his words falling on unreceptive ears. "You're not tougher than he was."

Before any more could be added, the reason for Pascoe's actions arrived. Somewhat red of face, breathing hard after making a hurried trip from the house of a charming, if somewhat free and easy, young widow, Lawyer Grosvenor entered the barroom. He skidded to a halt and stared down at Pascoe; shock twisted at his florid face as he turned to face Dusty.

"What happened?"

"He another of your clients, counselor?" Dusty countered.

"No—but he works for Mr. Bellamy, who is."

"It's like this, counselor," Mark put in. "That jasper ran head first into the wall."

"Why would he do that?" Grosvenor demanded.

"Grandstanding, I reckon. Trying to prove that he was tougher than your late marshal," Mark replied. "Which only goes to show, don't it?"

"What brings you here, counselor?" Dusty inquired. "Start closing the place down, Mark."

"Why?" the lawyer yelped.

"Two fellers who work here went after a cowhand who'd won a warbag full of cash bucking the tiger," Dusty explained. "Only my deputies caught them just after they busted the feller's head."

"So?"

"So they, the two jaspers, claim Bellamy told them to do it."

"They're lying!" Grosvenor stated without hesitation.

"Then why'd Bellamy run out in a hell of a hurry?" Dusty asked.

"He did not run out. He left on business and sent asking me to act on his behalf until he returns."

"That was kind of sudden."

"The whole affair is, and I rely upon your discretion, marshal, somewhat delicate," Grosvenor said. "You see, Mr. Bellamy has had a chance to invest in a business venture, the nature of which I am not at liberty to divulge right now. One of the stipulations of his acceptance being that he presented himself to the other principals at their convenience. So he arranged for me to act on his behalf, should he be called out of town hurriedly."

"And you don't know when he'll be back?"

"No."

"Nor where we can get in touch with him?"

"Why?"

"To clear him of the charges his men made."

"I'm afraid I don't know," Grosvenor replied, then looked to where Mark and the other deputies were circulating with word that the saloon was closing. "You can't close the saloon merely on unsupported charges by a couple of thieves!"

"That's not why I'm doing it," Dusty answered.

"Then why?"

"The Texas boy those two jumped's hurt real bad and he's mighty popular. If word gets out who jumped him— Well, this place's going to be in trouble."

"But surely you and your men can—"

"I can't tie down men in here," Dusty interrupted. "And I'm not chancing a riot starting. So I'm closing the place until it blows over."

"And when can it open again?" Grosvenor asked in the disgruntled tone of a man who knew he faced inevitable defeat. Nobody could blame a peace officer for taking even stern measures to prevent serious trouble.

"When I figure it's safe," Dusty promised, with an unspoken comment that the time would not be soon.

"How long do you reckon you can keep Bellamy's place closed, Dusty?" asked the Kid as they walked along the street on the morning after the attempted robbery.

"Long enough," the small Texan replied. "Say, how is that cowhand?"

"Waco went to see him like you said last night. The doctor allows that all he wants's a good rest, peace and quiet— Only that's not what he'll tell anybody else who asks."

"*Bueno*. As long as Grosvenor thinks the cowhand's likely to die, he'll warn Bellamy to stay away. Say, the doctor didn't strike me as a feller who'd be so all-fired obliging."

Being a stout Radical Republican, the doctor regarded the appointment of Texans, especially one with Dusty's Civil War record, as wrong. Not even after seeing the good work they did would he change his mind on the subject. So it came as a surprise for Dusty to learn that he had given willing cooperation to the deception.

With a broad grin, the Kid explained the medical man's change of heart.

"Now that depends," he said.

"What on?"

"Whether he reckoned the good ladies of Trail End'd stand for him making house calls at Annie's place and taking payment in trade. Only he don't reckon they will."

"That fixed the doctor," Dusty drawled. "But it won't keep Annie's bunch from talking."

"There's only Annie'll see him and she's not fixing to talk," the Kid replied. "See, when ole Waco put it to her the right way, she became all friendly and real eager to help."

"How do you mean, the right way?"

"Seems like he told her that you'd close her down to stop other fellers getting whomped on their heads going there, if she acted any other way. Then he allowed it's make you a whole heap friendlier happen she helped us."

"That kid!" Dusty ejaculated. "Have you been training him, Lon. He's getting as tricky as an Indian."

"He's sneaky enough to be a white reservation agent," the Kid corrected.

A group of businessmen were gathered on the sidewalk outside the First Chance Saloon, studying the front of the building. Dusty recognized them all as men, honest enough in themselves, waiting to see if he could break the corrupt influences before chancing their futures by coming to his side of the fence. Knowing just how much difference the support of such men could mean, Dusty studied them. With a feeling of pleasure, he noticed the smiles and friendly nods which had been noticeably absent during the first days.

"Howdy, Cap'n," greeted Titmuss. "Do you reckon Bellamy'll be back?"

"I couldn't say," Dusty answered, halting on the street and facing the men. "Is something bothering you?"

"He owes some of us money," put in a leathery-faced Scottish businessman. "We was wondering—"

"Mr. Grosvenor's acting for him while he's away," Dusty told the men. "Likely he'll—"

While Dusty was talking, the Kid turned and looked around him. So far nobody had tried another murder attempt, since Jackley's death, but that did not mean the danger was over. So the Kid remained alert, doing his duty by watching Dusty's back.

Nor did he confine himself to examining the street for possible danger. Out beyond the town, the country rose in a broken, gradual slope with plenty of cover that a would-be killer might hide among. Working swiftly and methodically, the Kid searched the land before him. Starting with the foreground, he scanned every rock, clump of bushes and fold in the ground from left to right. Even as he concluded that his caution was groundless, something flickered farther up than he expected. At the extreme top of his vision, the tiny dance of light still drew his full attention. Unless he called the turn wrong, that flicker was caused by the sun reflecting on a piece of glass. Except that no piece of glass ought to be among the clump of chokeberry bushes. With that point established, examined and understood, the Kid took the necessary action.

"Drop!" he snapped, giving what amounted to a whole volume of instructions under the circumstances.

Instantly, without a single thought for the dignity of his office, Dusty obeyed. Years of riding danger trails at the Kid's side had given the small Texan the greatest respect for his ability. Experience had long since taught Dusty to act, not hesitate or hold debates as to the reason, when that urgent note came into his companion's voice.

Nor did the warning come a second too soon. Even as he started to drop to the ground, Dusty heard an eerie hissing crack above him. Then something tore the Stetson from his head with considerable force and a cloud of splinters erupted out of the edge of the sidewalk.

"Wha—!" Dusty began, breaking his fall with his hands.

"Stay down like they've got you, *amigo!*" the Kid hissed urgently, acting like a man who had just seen his best friend shot, and tried to locate the killer.

So close had the bullet come that the businessmen on the sidewalk believed it had struck Dusty. Leaping forward, they added to the scene the Kid wished to present should the distant marksman still be watching. Although he knew that another bullet might come, with him as its mark, the Kid turned and sprang towards where Dusty lay. Then the men gathered around and partially obscured the Texans from view.

"Did they get you, Cap'n Fog?" Titmuss gasped.

"No," Dusty answered, without moving. "But make like they did. What was it, Lon? I didn't hear a shot."

"You wouldn't, where it was fired from," the Kid replied. "One of you fellers act like you're going to fetch the doctor."

"Doc—!" began the Scot, staring at the Kid and then to Dusty's undamaged but recumbent frame.

"Do it, Angus!" Titmuss barked, showing a surprising grasp of the situation. "Run down the street, into the doctor's office; he's not there but stay inside for a spell."

"Aye, I'll do that," the other answered and departed on the run.

"Now some more of you look around, like you're trying to see where the shot came from," Dusty requested. "After that, pick me up and carry me down to the office. Lon, watch yourself. He may try for you next."

"Keep us between you and him, Kid," Titmuss put in and grinned as one of the other men let out a startled exclamation. "Don't worry. It's not us that jasper out there's after."

While the would-be killer might not be watching, Dusty intended to take no chances. If the man was still keeping them under observation, he must see everything to make him believe his bullet found its target. Certainly it had come close enough for the deception to have a better than even chance of working. So Dusty lay limp and allowed the townsmen to raise him from the ground. Holding him in such a way that they hid his head from the marksman's sight, the men carried him along the street.

The Kid kept on the inner side of the group, presenting too uncertain a target for another attempt at wiping out the local law. As he walked along, his eyes studied the terrain and pinpointed the place from which the shot had come. By the time the party reached the office, he felt sure that he could find the spot where the killer was hiding. If the man should still be there—the Kid hoped that he would be.

"Get back inside!" the Kid snapped as Mark and Doc burst from the office. "It's all right."

Realizing that something urgent must be happening, the two deputies obeyed. They stood back and watched Dusty carried inside, then set on his feet after the door closed to hide the sight from the street.

"What the hell?" Mark demanded. "We thought—"

"Let's hope whoever shot at me thought the same," Dusty replied.

"I'll ask him," promised the Kid, walking to the wall rack and lifting down his magnificent rifle.

"Need help?" asked Doc.

"I've got all that I need," the Kid assured him, crossing to the desk and taking out a box of bullets. "You boys stay inside."

"How long?" Dusty asked.

"Until I get back, it'll be safer then."

"Here, Cap'n," one of the townsmen said, holding out Dusty's Stetson. "He sure made a mess of this."

Taking the hat, Dusty looked at the jagged gash in its crown. An icy hand seemed to touch him as he contemplated the effect and imagined what the result would have been if the Kid's warning had come an instant later. Forcing himself to ignore the thought, Dusty tossed the hat on to the desk.

"Sooner the hat than my head," he said.

Selecting a route that he hoped would keep him hidden should the marksman still be watching, the Kid made his way through the back streets to the livery barn which housed the floating outfit's horses. On arrival in Trail End, the

Texans discovered that it had been the barn's owner who first brought the state of affairs in the town to Governor Mansfield's attention. He also regarded their coming as a real blessing, so they did not hesitate to leave their horses and saddles in his care.

At the Kid's whistle, the huge white stallion loped across the corral as obediently as a well-trained hound-dog. Quickly he swung saddle and bridle into place, making all ready for the work ahead. Like most Texans, he fixed his saddle-boot at the near side and with its mouth pointing to the rear. Carrying it in such a manner placed the rifle in a perfect position to be drawn on dismounting. After sliding the Winchester into the boot, the Kid mounted and rode off in search of the man who had tried to kill Dusty.

Realizing that the marksman might still be watching, the Kid did not go in a direct line towards the clump of chokeberry bushes. That rifle in his boot had been specially selected at Winchester's factory for the extra accuracy of its barrel—then given the superb finish and, for once, modest claim "One of a Thousand"*—but it could not match the other man's weapon. Although the Winchester Repeating Arms Company supplied sights graduated to 1,000 yards, the Kid knew its rifles could not *accurately* cover half that distance. Light, compact, simple of operation and maintenance, the Winchester rifle excelled in its field. Shooting at eight hundred yards did not come into the same county as its field. If the Kid hoped to come through the time ahead, he must get much closer than half a mile before tangling with the marksman.

So he rode out of town on the opposite side to where the marksman had hidden. Once clear of the buildings, every vestige of the white man left the Kid and only the clothes remained. A pure *Pehnane* Comanche, one of the fabled Dog Soldier war lodge to boot, slouched easily in the white's

* Out of 720,610 Model 1873 rifles produced, only 124 received the title.

saddle. He traveled like any *Pehnane* warrior on such a mission, as inconspicuously as possible, alert, keen-eyed, taking advantage of every piece of cover to avoid being seen. All the time he aimed to reach the clump of chokeberry bushes.

Before approaching the bushes, he studied them from a concealed position. Satisfied that the marksman no longer remained in occupation, he advanced. Dropping from the saddle, he left the horse standing with the reins looped loosely around the horn. Tied or loose, the stallion could be relied upon to remain where he left it until needed.

Going forward, the Kid raked the ground ahead of him with his eyes, and read its message. He found with no difficulty where the man had lain to make the shot, locating the two holes left by the Y-shaped rack spiked into the earth and used to support the rifle's barrel while taking sight. Then, as added confirmation to his theories, he saw a long brass cartridge case lying among the bushes.

"Just like I figured," the Kid thought. "*Ka-Dih,* you've sure been good to me this day."

After the brief comment to the Great Spirit of the Comanche, the Kid walked back to his horse. Swinging astride, he rode around the bushes and found the marksman's tracks. At first the man had gone on foot to where a horse waited, then he swung into the saddle and rode off. The Kid followed on the would-be murderer's line. Before he had covered a hundred yards of the easiest tracking ever to come his way, a worried feeling began to grow on him.

"Was I a prideful man, Blackie," he told the horse, "I'd say that jasper was selling me mighty short as a sign-reader. Only nobody can say I'm a prideful man."

With that he gave a greater attention to the range ahead, although nobody who watched him would have thought such a thing from the relaxed manner in which he sat the big horse. Yet for almost a mile he saw nothing to cause him any concern and he passed through country well suited for the production of an ambush. Broken, rolling, its slopes splashed liberally with cover, the land traversed by the Kid spelled danger to him; more so when taken with that plain, too obvious trail the marksman left.

Going down a slope, the tracks turned along the bottom of a wide valley. Age-old instincts, coming from ancestors well-versed in the art of surprise, screamed warnings. Every fiber and instinct in the Kid's body tingled with expectation, ready for whatever lay ahead.

And something did!

Much closer than the Kid expected!

During his childhood among the Wasps, Quick Stingers, Raiders—or what other name the white brother's tongue gave to the *Pehnane* —the Kid excelled at one game in particular. *Nanip'ka,* Guess-Over-The-Hill, was the game which taught a young Comanche to locate hidden enemies. Schooled from an early age in its mysteries, the Kid doubted if any white enemy could beat his capable instructors in the finer points of hiding, or evade his well-trained scrutiny.

Thinking back on the matter, the Kid laid blame for what happened on the weapon used in the murder attempt. He was concentrating mainly on the distance, with only precautionary glances closer to hand.

To give him his due, the man lying behind a rock only a hundred yards from the Kid's position possessed a fair skill at concealment. He had selected a good place, lining the barrel of his weapon between the rock and a scrubby sassafras bush growing by its side. However he lacked one vital essential, patience. Moving slightly, possibly to ensure a better aim, he attracted the Kid's attention. Finding the enemy so close handed the Kid something of a shock, but did nothing to slow his reaction to the discovery.

Without a hint of warning, he pitched sideways from his saddle. There was no time to grab the rifle before going. The man being on the left slope called for a departure to the right, which further prevented the Kid from collecting his favorite weapon.

Flame spat from the ambusher's weapon, a bullet split

the air just above the Kid and the crack of the shot merged with the yell which broke from him. In leaving the saddle, he tapped the white's ribs with his toe. Immediately the horse loped off, veering away from the hidden man's position. Still in the air, the Kid twisted his right hand palm outwards about the butt of the Dragoon. When he lit down on the ground, he held the cocked revolver ready for use. However he could see no cover behind which he might hide.

"Looks like *Ka-Dih* figures he's done enough for one day," the Kid told himself bitterly. "And serves me right at that."

Then to the Kid's amazement, his assailant rose and started down the slope in his direction. For a moment the man's action numbed the Kid into immobility. An answer sprang to mind, one which made the Kid decide that *Ka-Dih* had not deserted his quarter-blood devotee.

Inching his head around, the Kid studied the man whose arrival at the First Chance the previous night had attracted Mousey's attention. Circumstances had prevented the informer from passing on his findings to Dusty, but the Kid drew much the same conclusions from the man's appearance.

Despite his clothing, the man failed to form a correct estimation of the situation. Or maybe he figured that he was dealing with a slow-moving white man instead of *Cuchilo*, grandson of Long Walker and a *Pehnane tehnap** in his own right. Thinking the Kid to be an ordinary cowhand, the man believed his bullet's arrival had caused the fall from the saddle. So he walked unconcernedly down the slope to either finish off the job, or rob his victim's body.

A wolf-savage grin twisted the Kid's face, wiping all semblance of youth and innocence from it. When he drew the Colt, he never expected such a piece of luck. So he prepared to make the most of it.

After the one quick glance, the Kid did not look towards the man. Instead he relied on his ears to tell him of the

* *Tehnap:* experienced warrior.

other's progress. Even wearing moccasins, the other stepped heavily enough for the Kid to gauge the distance separating them. The shot fired by the man had not come from the original weapon, of that the Kid felt certain. In fact he could make an accurate guess at the type of gun the other held. While it lacked the first's range, it still licked the Dragoon for distance.

The man's feet stopped moving. Instantly the Kid looked up and saw danger. At least thirty yards away, the attacker stood with his right foot on a rock, the Spencer carbine lifting to his shoulder.

Twisting his body over, the Kid rolled aside as the man shot. Lead struck the ground where his body had been a moment before and screamed off in a ricochet. Landing on his belly, the Kid gripped the Dragoon's butt in both hands. He rested his elbows on the ground to give a steady base for the four pound one ounce weight of the old gun. Already the man was beginning to work the Spencer's triggerguard lever, so there would be little enough time to spare.

Taking careful aim, the Kid squeezed the trigger and his Dragoon boomed awesomely. Through the smoke caused by igniting forty grains of prime du Pont powder, the Kid saw his attacker jerk as if struck by a sledgehammer. Not until smokeless powder, higher quality steel and the .44 Magnum caliber cartridges made their appearance would any handgun exceed the Dragoon's power; and the lower velocity, backed by the round, soft lead ball used by the Kid, gave the old Colt a manstopping potential that not even the big Magnum equaled.

Struck in the chest by the bullet, the man hurled backwards and spreadeagled himself on the ground, the Spencer flying from his hands. Coming to his feet, the Kid started to walk forward. His eyes went from the man, sure there would be no further danger at his hands, to the carbine.

"That damned saddlegun couldn't carry half a mile," he thought. "Which means he's got two guns, or there's another skin-hunter around. Which same brings up something real ticklish. Where at's this here other fe—"

An explosive snort burst from the stallion, chopping off the Kid's reflections on the affair. Darting a glance ahead, he saw the white standing with head thrown back and looking up the left slope. Without even waiting to see what had alarmed his horse, the Kid once more acted at top speed. Flinging himself to the right, he heard a bullet pass him, he dived over a rock, then wriggled rapidly behind a bush some feet from it.

"Now I know where that jasper is," he remarked with gloomy satisfaction.

Never a man who enjoyed the pleasures of outdoor life, Evan Bellamy hated the way in which he had been forced to spend the previous night. The saddle he used for a pillow possessed serious shortcomings, while he felt that borrowed blankets—which he suspected of already having been occupied—spread on the ground fell badly in comparison with the soft mattress and sheets of his bed at the First Chance. Brought out of town by Griswold, Lou Dancer's skinner, the saloonkeeper had spent a miserable night under the stars. The only bright spot of the business came with the news that the buffalo hunter had killed Dusty Fog earlier that morning. Cold, disheveled, wanting to back and resume control of his business, Bellamy even found a fault with that.

"I still don't see why you didn't stay put and get more of 'em," he said.

Dressed in much the same way as Griswold, although slightly cleaner, Dancer was a middle-sized, stocky man with thick wrists and powerful hands. Directing a contemptuous glance at the gambler, he gave a sniff and nodded to where a fine Sharps Old Reliable buffalo rifle rested on his saddle, a telescope sight fitted to it.

"I couldn't get a clear sight on him, and I don't waste lead through that rifle, either."

"But—"

"Look, mister," Dancer interrupted. "You hired me to

kill off them Texans. I wouldn't walk into your place and tell you how to rig a deck of cards. So don't you tell me my line."

"No offense," Bellamy replied, although the words almost stuck in his throat. He knew that he could not manage without Dancer at that moment and wished to avoid antagonizing the man.

"None took. I just likes to show how things lie. Sure, I could have shot. But I'd likely've missed, and that'd maybe let them find out where I was hid. So I let well alone. Maybe in an hour I'll go back and try for another one."

"Can't we have a fire?" Bellamy asked.

"Naw!" growled the buffalo hunter, his contempt even more plain. "We don't want smoke leading 'em out here."

"There's no chance of them finding us, is there?"

"Maybe. I left a nice clear trail from the bushes and put Gris to watch it. If they come, he'll let us know."

"Then what do we do?"

"Nail some more of their hides to the wall. You reckoned there'd be none of the town folks side them with Fog dead?"

"Not enough to worry over," Bellamy answered with assurance.

"Then we've only cowhands to worry about and I've never met one of 'em was any good for the sort of fight we'll make. That old gun of mine licks the hell out of the Winchesters they'll have."

"But suppose Griswold misses seeing them?"

"For a gambling man, you sure worry," Dancer snorted. "There ain't a white man any place can lick him at laying in wait."

The crack of a shot came to their ears and Bellamy whirled in the direction of the sound.

"That was old Gris' Spencer," Dancer commented, striding to where his rifle lay and picking it up. "Come on, let's take a look and see if I can collect any more of them bounties."

With that the buffalo hunter went bounding off. Not

wishing to miss the warning should Dancer's scheme fail, Bellamy followed on his heels. They ran up a slope, slowed down near the top and advanced at a more cautious pace. While they took care to avoid being seen, neither gave a thought to the wind being behind them and blowing over the rim. Flattening, down, the men inched forward until they could look over. Before they achieved their desire, the deep bellow of the Kid's Dragoon answered a second crack from Griswold's carbine. That caused them to increase their speed. Less skilled in such matters than Dancer, Bellamy exposed himself above the skyline.

Already alerted by the wind-carried scent of the men, the white stallion stood watchful as a wild animal. Seeing the sudden change in the sky-line's shape, caused by Bellamy's incautious appearance, the horse let out the snort that had warned its master of danger.

Despite its superb accuracy, the telescope-sighted buffalo gun failed to make a hit on the Kid. Capable of holding true at great distances, sighting it took time and it did not lend itself to snap-shooting. Dancer shot more in hope than expectancy and his marksman's inner sense told him that he had missed. Letting out a low curse, he watched the Kid disappear behind the rock but failed to see the change of position. However, certain points emerged from the brief sight of the Texan.

"He don't have a rifle with him," the buffalo hunter told Bellamy. "So if you move along there a piece and keep him busy, I'll soon fix his wagon."

"*I* don't have a rifle," Bellamy protested.

"Nor's he. All I want for you to do is throw lead down at him, it don't make no never-mind where it goes. You can leave the rest to me. Just do like I say."

Reluctantly Bellamy started to obey. His confidence grew as no shots came up in his direction and he watched Dancer settle down to lay a careful aim on the rock behind which their victim had disappeared. As long as the Kid did not have a rifle, he was at their mercy.

The same thought struck the Kid almost at the identical moment. Having seen Bellamy moving away from the buffalo hunter, he guessed the plan. Then he ignored the gambler as a factor, on the grounds that Bellamy's lack of a rifle made him a lesser menace than the Sharps-toting marksman.

Aware of the Sharps rifle's accuracy potential, the Kid also knew its limitation under the circumstances. Up to a range of two hundred yards, the distance from the Kid to Dancer, the Winchester possessed advantages over the other other weapon.

However the Kid did not hold his Winchester; it rode in the saddle-boot of his horse and a good seventy-five yards along the valley bottom. The dead man's Spencer was closer, but the Kid felt disinclined to risk his life on a strange weapon. Especially as he believed he could lay hands on the Winchester, happen *Ka-Dih* just handed out one last chance.

Moving carefully into a crouched position behind the bush, the Kid looked up the slope. Maybe that skin-hunter could toss straight lead, but he lacked in other even more vital respects. From what the Kid could see, Dancer still believed him to be behind the rock and was aiming accordingly.

"My thanks, *Ka-Dih!*" breathed the Kid. "You're sure sticking by me today."

That done, he gave a low, trilling whistle. Along the valley, the big horse tossed its head and started walking in his direction. While the men above saw it, they seemed to attach no importance to the white's actions. Nearer it came, the Winchester's black walnut butt pointing rearwards on the side nearest to the waiting Texan.

Another whistle, sharp, imperative, left the Kid's lips. Immediately the white's pace increased, changing from a slow, aimless-seeming walk to a run in a few strides. Dancer guessed what the Kid planned, or some of it, for he thought the other intended a dash forward, flying mount and full gallop to safety. So the Sharps lined on the rock from behind which the victim must come. At that distance he could make sufficient correction no matter which side the Kid appeared on.

Only the Kid did not come from behind the rock. Instead he shot into view some two yards away, hurling himself forward with the speed of a spooked pronghorn, yet with far more deadly intent than any fleeing pronghorn presented. Running man and racing horse converged while a cursing Dancer tried to correct his aim. Up lifted the rifle, to be ready to slice lead home when the Kid hit the white's saddle.

Instead of trying to mount the horse, the Kid ran by it. In passing, his left hand shot out, caught hold of the Winchester's butt and slid the rifle from the boot.

Just an instant too late Dancer saw what was happening and tried, again, to make a hurried change of aim. The Sharps' limitation, on which the Kid had gambled his life, showed all too plainly. Capable of hitting and knocking over a buffalo at up to a mile, its weight and length prevented rapid alterations to the point of aim. Blasphemy poured from Dancer's lips as he tried to settle the telescope on the Kid's fast-moving figure and found doing so far harder than aiming at a motionless buffalo bull.

White stallion and black-dressed man separated, the horse running on as the Kid dropped into a kneeling position. The Winchester flowed smoothly to the Kid's shoulder, lining upwards as his right eye peered along the barrel. Before Dancer could line the Sharps, flame lanced out of the repeater's barrel. For a fast-taken shot, the bullet flew true. It struck the buffalo gun under the breech, spinning the weapon from Dancer's hands. Pain and fury mingled in the yell which rang out. A mixture of the same emotions caused the man to lurch upwards and snatch at the revolver holstered at his right side.

Down flicked the lever of the Winchester, tossing an empty cartridge case into the air. Up it rose, sent by a deft twist of the Kid's wrist, to slide a loaded bullet into the chamber. A brief pause to change the line of sight and the Kid again tightened his finger on the trigger. Powder cracked, lead hissed through the barrel and towards its mark. Shocking pain tore into Dancer for a moment. Then his lifeless body, the back of the skull hideously torn where the bullet emerged, tumbled over and from the Kid's view.

Again the lever blurred, for the Kid had seen Bellamy moving along the rim, and he could not be certain if the saloonkeeper carried a rifle. Twisting around on his lowered right knee, the Kid swung the rifle in the direction where he had last seen Bellamy. Clearly the saloonkeeper did not intend to make a fight after watching Dancer's fate. All the Kid saw was the back of Bellamy's head disappearing rapidly from sight.

"It's not that easy, *hombre!*" he growled, rising and whistling.

After passing its master, the white had gone along the valley a short way and turned. The signal brought it back on the run and, before it stopped, the Kid went into the saddle like a coon hopping on to a log. Guiding the horse with his knees, he sent it leaping up the slope.

Bellamy ran fast, making for the camp where he could find the means of escape. Behind him lay two dead men, their mouths closed against giving testimony that he had hired them. If he could get clear, there might be a chance of Grosvenor clearing him of the charges laid by Baines and Croft. Dusty Fog might suspect who had hired the buffalo hunters, but could never prove it in a court of law.

Then he heard the rapid drumming of hooves. Throwing an anxious glance over his shoulder, he saw the huge white stallion top the rim. On its back sat a grim-faced man who still held the deadly rifle which had brought an end to Dancer's life. Bellamy needed only one quick glance to know he could not out-run the horse to the camp.

With that thought accepted, he turned and the Colt flashed into his hand. Some fifty yards separated them, too far for him to hope for better than a lucky hit. Being a gambler,

Bellamy never placed reliance on luck. So he made his decision. The horse offered a bigger target and when it fell might throw its rider hard enough to incapacitate him.

Seeing the gambler raise the revolver, the Kid guessed what he planned and acted to deal with the threat to his horse. With a lithe swing, he tossed his left leg over the saddle and jumped from the racing horse's back. Landing with an almost cat-like agility, although the white was running at a fast pace, he bounded off to one side. Bellamy's plans took a rapid revision at the sight. Turning the Colt away from the stallion, he tried to line it on the Kid. In doing so, he found himself between the devil and the deep blue sea.

On thundered the stallion, bearing down on the saloonkeeper with an intent directness which ought to have sounded a warning to him. No lover of open-air pursuits, Bellamy regarded a horse as nothing more than a means of traveling from one place to another when more comfortable transport was not available. So he lacked the kind of equestrian-savvy to know the danger. Figuring the main threat to his life was the Kid, he directed his full attention at the other. Adopting the classic target-shooting stance, the saloonkeeper aimed and waited until the Kid stopped, and turned and raised the rifle.

Suddenly Bellamy realized just how close the horse had come. But by that time it was too late. Letting out the savage fighting scream of a stallion defending a herd of mares, the big horse crashed full into the man. The impact sent Bellamy flying, his revolver barked as it spun from his fingers, then he landed on the ground. Just one scream broke from his lips as he saw the huge white rearing above him. Then steel-shod hooves slashed downwards, stamping home with all the power of a mighty, muscle-rippling body behind them. As the sickening thuds rose, Bellamy's scream chopped off short but the stallion did not halt its attack.

Not even the Kid could control his big horse at such a moment. All its wild, savage nature came to the fore and it reverted to the primitive state from which he had plucked it as a boy. Nor, if the truth be told, did the Kid feel sorry for the stallion's victim. In the days before the floating outfit came to Trail End, Bellamy had cheated, robbed and on two occasions killed trail hands. The First Chance Saloon ranked high on the list of complaints laid by indignant Texas trail bosses before the Governor of Kansas. Furthermore, Bellamy had hired the buffalo hunter to murder all the floating outfit—the Kid did not believe Dusty was to be the only victim—and had tried to kill the horse. To the Kid's eminently practical way of viewing the situation, simple justice was being done.

Advancing watchfully, the Kid spoke in a gentle, soothing manner to the snorting horse as it stood over the bloody wreckage of the saloonkeeper. Slowly the blood-wild fury left the stallion and it walked forward.

"You're going to need a good cleaning, Blackie hoss," the Kid said, patting its sleek white neck. "That's the worst of your color, things show on it."

Attracted by the noise, Lawyer Grosvenor crossed to the window of his office. What he saw sent him hurrying from the building and in the wake of the crowd that was escorting the Kid to the marshal's office. Leading four horses, three of which carried significant shapes draped over their saddles, the Kid headed something of a procession through town. Dusty and the other deputies came on to the sidewalk as their companion drew rein before the office building.

"It's done," he told them.

"Who were they?" Dusty asked, walking towards the horses and reaching up at the tarp covering one's burden.

"Bellamy and a couple of hide-hunters he'd hired to thin us out a mite," the Kid replied. "And I wouldn't uncover him out here, was I you. He tried to shoot ole Blackie and missed."

Having seen the white's work, Dusty accepted the hint. Better to leave the bodies until they were in the privacy of the undertaker's yard than to expose such a sight to the view of the crowd.

"What's happened?" Grosvenor demanded, thrusting his way through the crowd.

"You mind that business deal your client, Mr. Bellamy, went on, counselor?" the Kid asked, cold eyes raking the lawyer from head to foot.

"Y-yes," Grosvenor replied, darting worried glances at the horses.

"It just fell through," said the Kid.

PART FOUR

May's Try

Walking leisurely along Trail End's main street, Waco glanced at a wagon halted opposite Titmuss' general store. From its appearance, it might belong to a medicine show troupe of the kind that traveled the country peddling "all-healing" brews to the crowd gathered for the entertainment. A burly, middle-aged man with close-cropped hair and a flattened nose was standing at the outer horse's head. On the sidewalk, a shortish, slender man in a flashy town suit, derby hat, spats and shoes was talking with a couple more town dwellers.

The street being wide enough at that point for the wagon not to be causing an obstruction, it attracted only casual attention from the youngest of the town's deputies. Before he could come alongside and read the lettering printed on the canopy, he saw a girl approaching him. Small, but with the full-busted, slim-waisted figure much approved of at the time, she wore a wide brimmed, feather-decorated hat, traveling suit of somewhat brighter colors than "good" women sported, and carried a small grip.

"Hey, Ginger gal!" Waco greeted, walking forward. "Say, what brings you here. Is Babsy with you?"

Recognition appeared to be mutual, although the red-headed girl seemed more perturbed than pleased to see an old friend.

"H-hello, Waco," she said. "No. Babsy and I aren't together any more."

Studying the girl, Waco saw changes which surprised and puzzled him. When they last saw each other, Ginger had been on the verge of trying to break into the legitimate theater—as opposed to working in a saloon—in a "sister" singing act with the little blonde who had been Waco's first sweetheart.

Unless appearances lied, things must have gone wrong. While Ginger's clothes had cost good money, they showed signs of hard use and wear. Her lack of any jewelry also pointed to a change for the worse in her fortunes. Yet it was her face which told Waco most. In Mulrooney Ginger had been a pretty, vivacious girl with a merry smile and joy of life bubbling in her. Now her eyes were dull, with shadows under them and the full lips no longer smiled.

"You're not together, huh?" Waco inquired.

"No."

In the face of such a flat refusal to say more, Waco let the matter drop. Clearly Ginger did not want to talk about the split with Babsy, and Waco respected her desires. Yet he felt that he must learn more about her presence in town.

"You're here to work?" he asked.

"Sure," she replied, her voice dull if a touch defensive. "At the May Day Music Hall."

"There, huh?"

"Yes."

"On the stage, singing?"

"M-maybe," Ginger answered, looking down at her feet. "But back at the old game as well."

"May's theater's not like the Fair Lady in Mulrooney, Ginger gal," Waco warned gently.

"It's work," she replied. "And I n—"

Along the street, a window in Titmuss' store broke outwards and the sound of a shot from inside the building chopped off the girl's words. Letting out a scream of pain, the outer horse of the wagon team plunged, then sank down as the bullet which broke the window drove into its side.

"Stay put!" Waco ordered, vaulting the hitching rail and starting to run along the street.

Three saddled horses stood before the far end of the store, their reins hung across but not fastened to the hitching rail. Waco saw that and understood the implications. Letting out a bellow of rage, the burly man started across the street towards the store. Before he had taken three steps, a tall man in range clothes stepped from behind the far side of the horse. Bringing up a gun, the westerner fired. Struck in the chest, the driver spun backwards. A woman on the wagon let out a scream as the driver, blood-stain spreading across his collarless shirt's front, collided with the side and fell.

Then the westerner became aware of Waco's approach. Swinging around, he began to point his weapon in the deputy's direction. Down flashed Waco's right hand, fast despite the fact that he continued to run forward. Steel rasped on leather as the five and a half inch barrel of the off side Colt Artillery Peacemaker cleared the holster and roared. Shooting on the run, the youngster still planted home his bullet. Down went the man, his revolver flopping from his hand, but Waco did not have time to give the required attention to him.

Two more men in range clothes, their lower features masked with bandanas, burst from the store. Seeing Waco, the leader cut loose a fast shot, too rapidly taken for careful aim. Nor did the youngster remain motionless to offer a target. He went into the kind of rolling dive Dusty had taught him as a break-fall when pitched from a bucking horse. Landing on his left shoulder, he rolled straight over and back to his feet. Once up, the youngster adopted what would one day be called the gunfighter's crouch. Feet slightly apart, legs bent a little, spine slanting forward, the Colt held waist high and in the center of his body, the position allowed instinctive aiming and at close range could be deadly. Just how deadly showed when Waco fired his second shot. Although the man had already recocked his gun, he did not have time to use it. Waco's bullet hit him between the eyes, sending him backwards. Swerving aside, the third man allowed his companion to strike the wall of the building, from where he pitched face forward to the sidewalk.

Despite holding a gun, the third man did not offer to stand and fight. Instead he bounded off along the sidewalk, going away from his horse and in Ginger's direction. Knowing that the girl might try to halt the fleeing man, or be grabbed as a hostage, Waco did not hesitate.

"Hold it!" he shouted, bringing up the colt to eye level ready for use should the command be ignored.

It was. The man kept running. So Waco took aim and squeezed the trigger. Down lashed the hammer, driving its striker against the base of the waiting cartridge. Powder ignited, to propel the two hundred and fifty grains of shaped lead through the rifling grooves of the Colt's barrel and hurl it into the running man's hip. Giving a screech of pain, the man crashed down and his revolver left his hand to skid on to the street.

Walking towards the wounded man, Waco prepared to disarm him of the second revolver he wore. Behind the deputy, the first of the trio raised his head, then reached for the fallen gun. Just as his fingers closed on it, the woman on the wagon shrieked a warning that merged with Ginger's yell.

"Behind you, Waco!" the redhead shouted.

Whirling around faster than a scalded cat on a hot stove, Waco saw the danger. Again he went into the crouch, but he did not rely on thumb-cocking the Colt. Instead his left hand whipped across to drive back the hammer while his right forefinger depressed the trigger. Fanning in such a manner might not be conducive to accuracy on a target range, but no faster way existed of firing a single-action revolver which needed manual cocking for each slot. Certainly Waco did not have cause for complaint at the effectiveness of such a method. Three shots rolled out so fast that they could barely be told as separate sounds. Not one of the bullets missed its mark. Already wounded by the youngster's first shot, the man lifted erect under the repeated impacts. He stood for a moment, the gun trickling from limp fingers, then collapsed.

Once again Waco turned his back on the man, only this time he did not need fear another attack. So he gave his attention to the third man. Crouched against the store's wall, holding his leg between both hands, the wounded outlaw let out a wail that he surrendered.

Attracted by the sound of shooting, faces appeared at windows or doors. Mark, the Kid and Doc rushed from the office with guns in their hands. Coming from the building which housed the local newspaper, Dusty sprinted in the direction of his young deputy. Satisfied that there would be no more danger, people began to move towards the store. Pale and looking a mite shaken, Titmuss walked out of his place.

"Are you all right, deputy?" he asked, looking around.

"Sure, are you?"

"Yes. One of them took a shot at me when I walked in on them, but he missed. Then they run out."

"They hit one of those gents cross the street, Doc," Waco called. "You'd best see to him."

"How many were there, boy?" Dusty inquired as he came up.

"Three," the youngster replied.

"We don't need to start looking for any of them then."

"Nope," Waco agreed, then walked up to Ginger. "Thanks."

"I knew you hadn't seen him," she replied, face just a shade paler than before. "Well, I'd best go and say howdy to the new boss."

Something in the girl's voice told Waco she was not looking forward with pleasure to the experience.

"Look, Ginger, if you want to go—"

"I'll do fine here, thanks," she interrupted and turned to walk in the direction of the theater.

For a moment Waco stood watching the girl go, trying to decide what he ought to do. Then Dusty called his name and he swung around to rejoin his friends.

Until then Waco had not found time to look closely at the wagon. It seemed that he had guessed wrong about the medicine show aspect. On the side in large black letters were the words, "LONDON SID TUFTON'S SPORTING TROUPE. Pugilists & Wrestlers For the Crowned Heads of Europe."

A good looking, plump woman knelt by the wounded driver, her gingham dress old and travel stained. Up on the box stood a tall, burly young man in a town suit, and a beautiful young woman stylishly clad in the height of saloon fashion. Black haired, handsome apart from a crooked nose, the man looked near to nausea as he stared at the scene before him. Not so the girl, her full lips parted in excitement as she took in the sight with eager gaze. Coming around the front of the team, the dude from the sidewalk skidded to a halt. He had a thin, sharp face with a hint of foxy alertness about it and he glared at the wounded man after studying the dead horse. Then he turned his face to Dusty and waved a hand towards the man.

"How is he, Doc?" Dusty asked before the man could speak.

"Bad," Doc answered, kneeling alongside the driver. "The bullet'll have to come out *pronto*."

"Not much chance of that," one of the local onlookers put in. "The doctor went out of town just an hour back, headed for the Santer place."

"I'll sen—" Dusty began.

"There's no time for that," Doc growled. "Get him taken to the doctor's place and I'll do it."

"Here here now!" the smallish dude interjected, the words coming out as "'ere 'ere, nah." "I want a real doctor fixing him up."

"Happen you wait long enough to get one, he won't need fixing," Doc answered. "Mark, get somebody to help you tote him."

Raising a scared, tear-streaked face, the plump woman looked at Dusty. "Is—Can—Does—"

"Doc's taken bullets out before, ma'am," Dusty assured her. "You go along with him if you like."

Something in Dusty's calm voice and Doc's quiet manner of competence soothed the woman. She rose and stood back as Mark brought men to help carry the driver off. While plump, her body showed firm flesh and she moved with a light rubbery bounce when on her feet.

"Who is he, mister?" Dusty asked after the wounded man had been removed.

"Battling Ben Sexton, marshal," the dude answered in his strange, alien accent. "Leading contender for the British heavyweight boxing title— Reckon he'll live?"

"Like I told the lady, Doc's real good at taking bullets out."

"But it still makes me a man short for tonight's display."

"What display's that?" Dusty inquired, annoyed at the man's obvious lack of concern for the injured driver other than as how the wound affected himself.

"You've never heard of London Sid Tufton's Sporting Troupe?" demanded the dude indignantly. "Why we've held exhibitions—"

"Oh, fist fighters," Dusty interrupted.

"The very best pair of boxers this town'll ever see," the dude snorted. "And two of the finest lady wrestlers in the whole world. I'm Sid Tufton." Then the thought of his show's loss returned. "Why didn't your deputy stop 'em sooner?"

"I would have, if I'd known what was happening," Waco put in hotly, not caring for the other's callous preoccupation with the fate of the display. "Only those three fellers didn't come up and ask me if they could rob the store—"

"Easy, handsome," the beautiful girl put in, swinging agilely to the ground. "Sid always gets all hotted up when he thinks he might lose money."

"Shut it, Taffy!" Tufton yelped, swinging to face the girl. Then he turned back to Dusty. "I shouldn't've sounded off like that, but I'm contracted to put on the display and—well, May doesn't pay if I don't produce."

"You've got me and Fran," the girl pointed out. "And we're a better than fair attraction. Then you can get the rubes to challenge Ernie—"

"Yeah, yeah!" Tufton put in. "I know all that. Damn it, I've lost a hoss and fighter already, with nothing to show for it."

A mocking smile came to the girl's face, enhancing the slightly sullen look which the beauty masked at other times. She had a shapely figure, and knew it, and moved with easy grace.

"That's what I like about you, Sid," she said. "You're all heart."

"Damn it!" Tufton snorted. "I'm going to see May. You'd best go to the hotel with Ernie and get us some rooms. It looks like we're here for a spell."

"Now there's a feller I could get to dislike, happen I knew him better," Dusty said dryly as the promoter and his two performers left.

"I don't need to know him better and I don't like him now," Waco answered.

With that the two Texans started to attend to the formalities concerning the wounded and dead outlaws.

"How'd you mean, Dip and Cannon can't work here this time?" Tufton yelped, staring in a suspicious and surprised manner at May as they sat in the latter's private office at the rear of the theater.

"Just what I said," May answered. "There'll be no picking pockets in my place tonight, or any other night you're in town."

"Damn it, the last time—"

"The last time you came here, those damned beef-heads weren't holding the badges," May interrupted, guessing what annoyed the other. "It's not that I've got my own dippers, Sid. One complaint and that damned marshal'd have me padlocked before morning."

Looking at the theater owner, Tufton found himself believing what he heard. Yet it went opposite to everything he remembered of Trail End from previous visits. On the other occasions, he had met with no objections to the added refinement to his display. In addition to putting on boxing or wrestling bouts—either exhibitions between his own people, or challenge matches with local hopefuls—Tufton sold cheaply produced books teaching boxing or self-defense. Yet the take from the bouts and books did not approach that brought in by two important members of the troupe who never appeared as part of it. Dip and Cannon, the two men Waco had seen talking with Tufton by the wagon, traveled separately from the others, but mingled with the crowds which gathered, and picked pockets. Their loot, split forty-sixty to Tufton's advantage, produced the promoter's major source of income.

On previous visits, for a cut of the proceeds, the two pickpockets had been made as welcome as the rest of the troupe by May; and operated in comparatively safe conditions, for Marshal Jackley never interfered with such enterprises. That had been a major factor in Tufton's decision to visit Trail End. For some reason the promoter had failed to hear of the change in the town's law enforcement body and he found the news unpleasant when finally learning of it.

"Nobody ever caught either of them at it," he protested, averse to losing the profits.

"And they're not having a chance to in here," May stated. "If they come in, my boys'll heave 'em out. That Dusty Fog's got the damnedest way of learning things and I'm taking no chances."

"But—"

"I'm not arguing, Sid. Fog's just looking for a chance to close me and I'm not giving him it."

While not exactly true, for Dusty had no intention of bothering anybody who ran an honest business, the explanation satisfied May.

"Did you say Dusty Fog?" asked the promoter.

"He's the marshal."

"That short runt—?"

"Yeah, that short runt," agreed May.

"It figures, the muscles on him," Tufton breathed. "He's got as fine a build as I've ever seen. You maybe wouldn't notice it, but I know what to look for and clothes can't hide it from me."

"He licked Jackley with his bare hands," May remarked.

"Did he now?"

"Tossed him clear through the window of the jail, then beat the hell out of him when he went back."

"Can use his-self, can he?" Tufton said, half to himself.

"All of them can, except that damned 'breed—and nobody's been stupid enough to try making him prove it."

"They've got this town closed up good, huh?"

"It's so law-abiding since the Governor brought 'em in that you wouldn't know it."

"Reckon folks'd see me right if I got shut of 'em for you?" Tufton asked.

"I know some who would," May admitted.

"Would they go up to—five hundred—for each one of them I run out?"

"That's a whole heap of money, Sid."

"So's what you boys're losing each week that you have

to run honest," the promoter pointed out.

"You'll get your money," May promised. "*If* you do it. But Jordan and Bellamy tried and died when their plays went wrong."

"They did?"

"Sure. And I don't want anything coming back on me."

"It won't," Tufton said, after thinking for a time. "You've spread the word that my lot're coming?"

"Of course I have," snorted May. "The railroad crews'll be in town to see the fights."

"Then I reckon I can do it," Tufton stated and explained his plan.

Although he saw how parts of the idea might work, May showed little enthusiasm for it.

"You'll never get any of 'em to go for it," he said.

"That young 'un who shot them owlhoots might, handled right. He acted real matey with your new gal."

"Which new gal?" demanded May suspiciously.

"The redhead. I was talking to Cannon and Dip on the street when I saw them. It started me wondering, seeing him wearing a deputy's badge."

Rising from his seat at the desk, May crossed the room and opened its door. "Hey!" he called to a passing stage-hand. "Go tell that new gal, Ginger, to come in here."

"Sure, boss," came the reply.

Neither of the plotters discussed their affairs further while waiting for Ginger's arrival. At last she entered the office, looking worried and just a touch frightened. Already some of the other girls had given her an inkling what kind of place she was working in, also about the conditions in the town. So she wondered if her meeting with Waco had been noticed. That sly-faced little dude had seen her talking with the deputy and had studied her in an interested manner on entering the theater as she went to the upstairs female quarters.

"How'd you like it here, Ginger?" May inquired.

"It's all right," she answered in a non-committal tone.

"Where'd you work before you went East?"

"The Buffalo and Fair Lady in Mulrooney."

"You'd be there when Dusty Fog held the badge then?"

"Yes," Ginger replied.

"Did you know him?" May asked.

"I saw him around, spoke to him a few times is all."

"How about his deputies?" Tufton put in. "You know any of them?"

"I met them all at one time and another," Ginger admitted cautiously.

"Including the young one, Waco?" May asked, trying just too hard to sound casual.

"Sure, I knew him," Ginger agreed. "He was sparking with one of the gals at the Fair Lady."

"I bet you're wondering what this's all about, gal," May commented.

"Well— Yes, I am," the girl replied.

"Look, Ginger," May said, putting on his most jovial and winning manner. "It's like this here. Things've been rough hereabouts for a spell and I reckon those Texans've picked up some wrong ideas about me. You could maybe help me get on to better terms with 'em."

"I'll try," Ginger promised, wondering just how serious her new employer might be. "Is that all, Mr. May?"

"Sure. Go and settle in. I want you helping out downstairs tonight."

Watching the girl leave, Tufton nodded in satisfaction. The idea he had partially formed seemed to have a better than fair chance of working in the light of what he now knew.

"She knew him well enough for him to try and help her," the promoter stated after the door closed. "I know now just how to work it."

"Can you rely on your folks to play along?" May asked.

"There's only Taffy and Ernie to worry about," Tufton assured him. "And that pair'll do anything—if the price's right."

• • •

Although Waco and Mark wore their badges, they did not attend the May Day Theater in any official capacity. It being their night off watch, they went along to the theater with the intention of spending an evening enjoying the show. Although Waco saw Ginger, he did not find a chance to converse with her. As soon as he and Mark entered the main room, May bore down on them and insisted that they share his table at the side of the boxing ring erected in the center of the floor.

Drawn in by the posters advertising Tufton's troupe, townsmen, buffalo hunters and trail hands gathered at the theater. By far the largest proportion of the audience consisted of gandy-dancers and other railroad workers. While the others, especially the cowhands, regarded fist-fighting as something of a novelty, the railroad men looked on it as an absorbing pastime and interesting sport.

Of course none of the various factions found anything to complain at with the first part of Tufton's show, a wrestling match between the beautiful, blond haired Taffy Davies and the older brunette, Fran Murkle.

Knowing something of the finer points of wrestling, Mark decided that he might have seen more scientific bouts, but never one with so much appeal for the audience. Whoever trained the women knew his business, and also possessed a keen idea of what the mass of male customers liked to see. The women wore sleeveless bodices, tights and pumps. Such an outfit set off Fran's plump figure to its best advantage but it was nothing compared with the younger, more beautiful blonde's attraction. On arrival in the ring, Taffy had shrugged off the blanket draped around her and turned slowly so that every man in the room could stare his goggle-eyed approval at her gorgeous figure.

Nor did the women rely solely upon looks to carry through the bout. They went into wrestling throws and holds with skilled precision. Maybe to Mark's trained eyes the various exchanges clearly had been practiced as a routine, but few of the other spectators realized it. Sympathetic applause rose when Fran took the first fall and rousing cheers greeted Taffy pinning the older woman to even the score. Then, after about a minute of the final round, something went wrong and showed Taffy in a far less sympathetic light.

Despite working to a routine, the women's efforts imposed a strain on them. Flipped over by Fran's flying mare throw, Taffy failed to break her fall correctly. Instead she hit the canvas with a thud that jarred a gasp of pain from her. The blonde's face flushed red and angry as the crowds laughed at her discomfort. Coming to her feet, she rubbed her rump and went towards Fran with a tight-lipped determination. For a moment they circled, adopting the classic ready stance of the catch-as-catch-can wrestler as they sparred for an opening.

Suddenly Taffy lunged in, both hands clamping around Fran's left wrist. Bracing herself, the blonde swung and hurled her opponent across the ring. Unable to stop herself, Fran went backwards into the ropes and they sagged out under her weight's thrust. Then the powerful springs which held the ropes taut contracted and propelled her towards the ring center.

Leaping forward, Taffy drove her knee sideways into Fran's stomach. Agony twisted the brunette's face at the impact and the breath burst from her lungs. She clutched at her stomach, staggered by the blonde and dropped to her knees facing a corner. Like a flash Taffy turned and kicked Fran between the shoulders, sending her head first into the padded turnbuckle hung over the ropes at the corner.

Bouncing back, Fran flopped to the floor. For a few seconds she lay still, then forced herself on to hands and knees. Shaking her head and looking dazed, the brunette rose. She staggered, looking at Tufton, who acted as referee, in a pleading manner.

Before the promoter could say anything, Taffy thrust him aside and attacked again. She threw the groggy-looking older woman, slamming her down to the canvas harder than previously. Three times the blonde, wild-eyed and screaming curses, dragged Fran up and threw her again. Nor did the older woman break her falls with the earlier ease, but lit down hard. Only the fact that the ring had padding under the canvas saved Fran from serious injury.

Shoving the scarcely protesting Tufton away, Taffy bent and took a double-handed hold of Fran's hair. She hauled the dazed woman erect and released her hold to leave Fran tottering on wobbling legs, gasping in pain and trying to appeal to the referee. Watched by the now silent crowd, Taffy ducked down to catch Fran's right ankle in her hands. Stepping back a pace, the blonde tugged the trapped leg up, causing Fran to tumble backwards to the mat. Before the brunette could protect herself, Taffy twisted her on to her face. Quickly Taffy pivoted around and back, until she stood astride Fran's torso with the woman's right leg bent upwards and trapped under her right arm.

Cries of pain broke from Fran as the agony of the hold tore into her leg and spine. Still Taffy retained the hold, applying extra pressure despite Tufton's orders to let go. Running forward, the two men trained as seconds—they had been sent on ahead to the theater while Tufton talked to his pickpockets—caught hold of the blonde and forced her to release the hold. For a moment she struggled, then relaxed, threw back her head and laughed in the direction of the sobbing Fran who crawled weakly to the edge of the ring.

Silence followed Taffy's victory, then Tufton raised the girl's arm over her head.

"The winner of the third and deciding fall, Taffy Davies!" he announced. "And your sympathy for a good loser, gents!"

At first only a desultory applause greeted the announcement, for the audience had been shocked by the blonde's unexpected display of pure violent, vicious temper. Slowly Taffy turned, arms raised, the tight clothing showing off every line of her gorgeous figure. As the seconds helped Fran from the ring, Taffy paraded around it. Then the blonde came to a halt, glaring across the room. Letting out a hiss of annoyance, she swung through the ropes, dropped to the floor and stalked towards the door through which the performers made their appearance.

Guessing something was going to happen, the audience watched the blonde as she headed for a table alongside the door. Dressed in a knee-long, garish frock, Ginger stood laughing and talking with the big young boxer. Suddenly the girl realized they had become the center of attraction and sensed trouble as Taffy came stamping towards them.

"All right, calico cat!" the blonde spat out. "Beat it!"

Surprise caused Ginger to remain at the man's side. During the afternoon she had met Ernie and been flattered by his attentions, yet she attached no great importance to them. Even the fact that he seemed to seek her out during the wrestling bout and insisted on buying wine for her failed to make her believe anything might develop out of the affair. Certainly she did not hope to gain anything from him and the blonde's attitude amazed her. It also raised Ginger's stubborn streak and caused her to act hastily.

"Who do you think you're talking to?" Ginger demanded.

"I'm talking to you!" Taffy shouted back, conscious that every eye in the room was fixed on them. "Every damned town I go to, some lobby-lizzy starts mauling my man. Well, I'll show you what they get!"

With that Taffy lashed around a slap that sent Ginger staggering into the wall. Despite the various tribulations that had come her way after breaking up the act with Babsy, Ginger's old temper remained. While she had worked in saloons for a few years, at no time had she ever qualified for the title lobby-lizzy; for that meant a prostitute.

Bouncing off the wall, she ducked her head and charged forward to butt the blonde in the body. Taffy had not expected such an immediate, or devastating response. So the surprise helped the force of impact to throw her backwards and she thudded down on to her rump. Still wild with fury, Ginger flung herself on to the other girl. Digging her fingers into the blond hair, the little saloongirl raised then thudded Taffy's head on to the floor.

"Stop 'em!" May bellowed, leaving his table and charging across the room.

Accompanied by yells demanding that the fight should go on, two of the saloongirls rushed forward to drag a screaming, struggling Ginger from Taffy. The blonde lay weakly writhing, mouth open and working soundlessly, eyes glazed.

"Lemme at her!" Ginger squealed, struggling in the grasp of the two bigger girls. "Call me a lobby-lizzy, would she!"

By that time every man in the room had stood up, those at the rear mounting chairs and tables to obtain a view. Mark and Waco rose an instant too late to follow on the theater owner's heels, for the crowd closed in behind him. Wanting to prevent trouble, they started forward and forced their way through the crush of excited men. Once a brawny gandy-dancer turned, scowling furiously, but he held down his comments and edged aside. Nor had it been just Mark's bulk and the deputies' badges that caused him to change his mind. Realizing that the other girl was Ginger, Waco wanted to reach her. The cold, grim expression on his face warned the gandy-dancer that any man who stood in the youngster's way might rapidly come to regret it.

Despite the reluctance of its members to consciously oppose their passage, Mark and Waco took time to push through the crowd. By the time they reached the center of attraction, a groggy looking Taffy stood facing Ginger who was still being held by the other girls. As the blonde shook her head and started towards the redhead, May moved forward.

"Hold it, Taffy!" the theater owner ordered, catching her by the arm. "I'm not having barroom cat-clawing in my place. If you want to fight her, get back into the ring."

Shock came to Ginger's face as she took in the implications of the offer. Already the hot-headed anger had died and she could understand just how lucky she had been. Only the fact that her butt had taken the blonde by surprise had prevented her from being soundly thrashed. In an all-in hair-yanking fight Ginger might stand a chance against the taller, heavier and stronger Taffy. Put her in the ring and the blonde had every advantage.

"'Ere, 'ere!" Tufton put in, worming through the crowd and advancing before either girl could reply to the offer. "That's not on, you know. My gal's just had a hard bout. She don't go into the ring again tonight."

Mutters, growing to shouts of disapproval rose from the crowd at the thought of such a novel treat being denied them. After a glance to make sure Waco could hear, May turned and raised his hands to silence the protests.

"Hold it, boys!" he called. "Like Mr. Tufton says, it wouldn't be fair to put his gal in the ring again tonight. So I say that we leave it until tomorrow night, if the ladies are agreeable."

"Agreeable!" Taffy shouted. "I'll take that fat-gutted alley cat any time."

"How about it, Ginger?" demanded May.

"That's out," Waco put in leaving Mark's side.

"I'm not sure how you come to be mixed in this, deputy," May replied. "I'd say it's up to Ginger to decide."

"Tell him 'no' Ginger gal," Waco ordered.

"You can say 'yes' or 'no'," May went on, looking pointedly at the girl. "I don't mind which—but the customers might and I can't keep on a gal who makes trouble."

"You mean if she doesn't fight, she's fired?" Mark asked, his every instinct warning of a trap.

"I'd have to let her go, deputy," May answered. "There'd be no other way."

Under the evenly spoken words lay a threat apparent only to Ginger and May. After splitting up with Babsy, Ginger had tried to continue as a single act. She lacked the talent to succeed on her own, but ran into debt before accepting the fact. When a booking agent offered her a way out, she accepted it before thinking of its full implications. In return for sufficient money to cover her debts and expenses, she signed a contract agreeing to work at the May Day Music Hall until paying off the advance—plus interest.

Too late Ginger realized her exact position, that she was almost a slave to May for an indefinite period. One of the things the agent impressed on her, after she signed the contract, had been the fate of anybody who abused his generosity. As long as May sent her payments in regularly, all would be well. If they stopped, or she left his employment, Ginger could expect to be found and marked for life. So she knew that she could not refuse May's demand.

"I—I'll take her on," Ginger faltered.

"You don't have to," Waco told her.

"The crowd's not going to like being cheated out of a fight, deputy," May pointed out and a rumble from the onlookers confirmed his words.

"Maybe the awficer would like to substitute for the gal, seeing's how he's so interested," Tufton put in. "If he would, my boy, Ernie Wotjac there'll be only too 'appy to oblige."

With a cold, sinking sensation Mark realized that a trap had been closed on Waco. Suddenly the blond giant saw everything in its true perspective. Each move of the affair had formed part of a plan to lead Waco into a dangerous situation. If the youngster refused the challenge, his position in town would be ruined. Should he accept, Mark did not doubt what the result would be.

While Waco equaled Wotjac in height, the other had weight and experience on his side. Given the full run of an all-in brawl, Waco might stand a chance; for both Dusty and Mark taught him much in the art of rough-house self-defense. Once in that boxing ring, the youngster would be restricted by rules which he imperfectly understood and matched against a trained boxer on the other's own terms.

"Don't do it, Waco!" Ginger pleaded. "I'll take her on."

"Just let her!" Taffy spat out. "I'll cripple her for life."

And if the expression on the blonde's face was anything to go by, she meant every word. Waco remembered how

Taffy handled Fran for doing far less than Ginger had. If the little redhead went into the ring, she might easily come out a cripple. There could be only one answer.

"She doesn't go into the ring, *hombre,*" the youngster stated.

"If you say so, *deputy,*" May answered. "A man in my position can't start arguing with the town law."

"The law's got nothing to do with it," Waco answered, seeing the scowls directed his way by various members of the crowd. "You know damned well that Ginger doesn't stand a whoop-in-hell's chance against that gal."

"She did all right just now," May pointed out, exultant at the way Waco was going deeper into the trap.

"Sure, she took the other gal when Taffy wasn't looking for it—"

"You've an easy way of saving her, awficer," Tufton put in loudly. "One any red-blooded gent'd take if he was so keen to help a gal. I reckon the folks'll settle for seeing you face Ernie."

Again the crowd rumbled their approval and agreement. While watching the girls might be a novelty, none of the audience expected her to put up more than a token resistance against the heavier blonde. Already Waco had proved himself capable of holding his end in a brawl. So he ought to offer a better show than the girls.

"Come on, deputy!" called a man from the depths of the crowd. "Put up, or cut out."

"You take him for the gal's sake, deputy," another voice yelled.

"Where do we talk, Ginger?" Waco asked.

"You don't mind him talking to her first, do you?" Mark demanded, facing the theater owner.

May did mind, on a number of grounds, but he knew better than put his objections into words. So far the plan was working every bit as well as he hoped. There seemed no way that Waco could refuse and retain any standing in town. Even the Texans would have no respect for a man who refused to fight if doing so would save a woman—even a saloongirl—from trouble. Thinking fast, May decided that allowing the private conversation would do no harm. Even if the girl told the full story, it would only strengthen the need for Waco to defend her. Then a flash of inspiration hit the theater owner.

"I'll put up a purse of two hundred and fifty for the winner and a hundred for the loser," he said. "Go talk to her in my office, deputy."

Watched by every occupant of the big room, Waco and Ginger crossed to the office and went inside.

"All right," he said, closing the door and turning to face the girl. "I want to know it all."

"Wh-what do you mean?"

"How come you got mixed up with that big jasper, knowing Taffy was his gal?"

"I didn't know she was!" Ginger objected. "She never come near him all the time we was talking this afternoon, or earlier on in the passage near the dressing rooms come to that. Hell, Ernie was nice to me, I never thought—"

"Then why're you so set on getting busted up bad?" the youngster growled. "That gal's mean and trained up real good. She's not Babsy and she won't stop by yanking out a few curls. You saw the way she whipped that gal over in the ring."

"It's you or me, Waco," the girl told him. "Ernie'll whip you bad if you go in against him."

"You don't have to face her," Waco pointed out. "Say no, nobody'll blame you for it."

"May'll fire me if I do."

"So then you go back to Mulrooney—"

"It's not that easy!"

"The hell it's not. Just go back and see. Sure the others might hooraw you about it, but they'll soon forget."

"That's only one of the reasons I can't go back," Ginger replied, for thinking of the catty comments that would greet her return had contributed to her remaining in the theatrical profession instead of going back to Mulrooney and her old job.

"Then go find another town and a straight saloon."

"I can't do that, either."

Taking the girl's hands gently in his, Waco forced her to look straight at him. "What happened between you and Babsy?"

Slowly, hesitantly, the story came out. At first the "sister" act went well. Their bounce and vitality, backed by Babsy's considerable talent, pleased all kinds of audiences and they rose rapidly to the top of the bills. Then a juggler who was appearing in a lesser capacity on the same bill began to make a play for Babsy. Learning something of his true nature, Ginger tried to warn her friend. Infatuated by the man, Babsy refused to listen and a blazing quarrel between them caused the act to dissolve.

"I should've kept my mouth shut," Ginger admitted tearfully. "But he was no good and Babsy's only a kid."

"Likely," Waco answered. "What happened to you after that, apart from not being able to find work and running real short of cash?"

"I didn't know my lack of talent showed that much," Ginger said in a bitter voice.

"You come to town wearing what's likely your only set of clothes and without as much as a glass ring. It didn't take much figuring to guess you'd come close to the blanket, gal."

"You're right. It's facing it that hurts. Babsy said it was her who sold the act—and she was right."

"You know Babsy," Waco said. "Get her riled and she'd breathe smoke 'n' fire at you. But she'd kiss and make up give her a chance."

"She was doing so well as a single that I wouldn't go back," Ginger sighed.

Then she told him the rest of the story, watching the anger lines grow on his face as she revealed the extent of the contract.

"If I quit here, or get fired, Bernstein back in Philadelphia won't be paid and he'll send somebody after me," she finished.

"Go to Mulrooney and say the hell with him," Waco suggested. "Miss Freddie and Buffalo Kate'll stand by you."

"They'd have nothing but trouble," Ginger answered. "Bernstein daren't let a girl get away with that, or the others'll start doing it."

"How much do you owe him?"

"Two hundred and fifty dollars—"

"Which's what May's offering for the winner of the fight," Waco breathed. "Lord, I've been *loco* not to see it before—And I've played right into their stinking hands."

"Waco!" Ginger gasped as the youngster released her and swung towards the door. "Don't be a fool. If you go into the ring you'd have as much chance against Ernie as he would facing you with a gun in his hand."

Just about to leave, Waco came to a sudden halt. His hand froze on the door handle and he stood like a statue for a moment. Then he turned, walked up to the girl, placed his hands on her shoulders and kissed her gently.

"You never said a truer word," he said.

Silence dropped on the room as Waco, followed by Ginger, left the office. Parting, the crowd allowed them clear passage to where Mark stood with Tufton and May. Ernie sat at the table, but shoved back his derby hat and rose as the youngster approached. The boxer would not be entering the ring until later, and so wore his town suit instead of his fighting outfit. The clothes did nothing to hide his brawny physique. Everybody could see his advantage in weight and heft over the young Texan. Yet Ernie hoped that the challenge would be met. Before agreeing to take part in the scheme, he had demanded two hundred and fifty dollars. Easy money, to the boxer's way of thinking, for beating the inexperienced deputy to a pulp.

"What about it, awficer?" Tufton asked in a loud voice.

"Is it you, or the gal we see?"

"Me," Waco replied and heard Ginger's gasp despite the rumble of excited comment that arose. He waited until silence dropped again before continuing, for he wanted every word to be heard. "That's a real good edge you're carving for yourself, *hombre*. A trained fister like him'd lick me easy, fighting his way— Only we won't be."

"I don't follow you," Tufton said in a puzzled tone.

"We fight *my* way," Waco explained and looked at Mark. "Go put one of your Colts on the table in front of that feller, cock it, then step back."

A stunned hush wiped out every last sound in the room as its occupants took in the full meaning of the youngster's words. Shock twisted Ernie's face and May let out a low hiss of frustrated fury.

"'Ere," Tufton gasped, first to recover his voice. "What's the game?"

"It's no game, *hombre!*" Waco answered. "Way I see it, this whole deal's been rigged to help run us out of town. Either I get into the ring and busted up bad, or have to run out with my tail dragging. Of if Dusty and the others cut in, some folks might figure on stopping them. To me, that's like a feller coming to town hunting me with a gun. When that happens, I meet him and see it through to the end. Put the gun there, Mark."

"Not mine, boy," Mark answered, face showing none of the pride he felt in the way the youngster turned the tables on May. He looked at a buffalo hunter met in Mulrooney, a man who respected the floating outfit's brand of law-enforcement. "Is your gun loaded, mister?"

"I've never yet walked around with an empty cylinder, deputy," the man replied. "That'd be plumb foolish."

Which figured to anybody who knew firearms and the conditions in range-country towns. So none of the crowd doubted that Ernie would receive a weapon loaded and ready for use; which they might if the gun came from Mark's holster.

"Put it by his right hand, cocked and with the barrel pointed this way," Waco ordered.

"It's your play, deputy," the hunter answered, drawing the Cavalry Peacemaker from its holster, thumbing back its hammer and placing it as directed on the table before Ernie, then stepping back hurriedly. "Like he said, young feller, that brings the odds more even—and still leaves you one hell of an edge."

True enough on the face of the matter. Cocked ready for use, its barrel pointing towards Waco, everything seemed to be in the boxer's favor, for the deputy's guns still hung in their holsters. All Ernie needed to do was drop his hand to the Colt's butt, lift it and fire.

"Go to it when you want," Waco told him.

Sucking in a breath, Ernie began to make either a move for the gun, or a gesture towards it. Instantly, without waiting to discover which, Waco acted. His right hand flashed back to the staghorn handle of the off side Colt, thumb coiling around the hammer, three fingers turning under the butt, the forefinger extended as the weapon started to rise from leather. While the gun still lifted, the thumb cocked the hammer, then slid from it to firing position around the top of the butt. Not until the barrel slanted towards the boxer did Waco's forefinger enter the triggerguard. For all that, a mere .6 of a second after the youngster's first movement, the Colt crashed and its bullet spun Ernie's derby from his head.

Shock and fright showed on the boxer's face as he stumbled back from the table. Twirling on Waco's forefinger, the smoking Colt slapped into the holster and his hand lifted from the butt.

"Try again, *hombre!*" the young Texan said.

Sweat poured down Ernie's face and he breathed in deeply, eyes fixed on Waco's grim-set features. In the ring no man had ever frightened the young boxer and he had given brutal beatings to a number of opponents less skilled than himself. It would have been the same if the plan had gone correctly, with Waco the victim. Only the Texan had turned the tables in no uncertain manner. Now he had the experience, the training which exceeded that of his opponent.

Almost as if it were happening again Ernie saw the scene in the street, when Waco's gun-skill had saved his life. Two men had died and another carried a wound due to that blond youngster's deadly ability. There had been a merciless efficiency in the way Waco dealt with the robbers that shocked the Eastern-born boxer.

Cold fear gripped Ernie. He did not doubt that the next time Waco drew would see a bullet crashing into his skull. For a moment he stood, staring at the tall young Texan, then he gave a hoarse cry and fled from the room.

Talk rumbled up as the boxer tore open the door and disappeared through it. Yet the affair was not over. Swinging towards Tufton, Waco pointed to the table.

"You like setting up fights, *hombre,*" the youngster said in a voice which chopped off all other conversation. "Now let's see how you stand up to one. The gun's on the table. Go pick it up."

"Wha—!" the promoter began.

"You take pay for setting fellers and gals to fighting. So let's see just how good you fight yourself."

"Me—I—"

"Count to five slow, Mark," Waco said. "And when you get to it, I'm making my play."

"One!" Mark said.

"'Ere—!" Tufton squawked.

"Two!"

"You ca—"

"Three!"

"May! You can't—"

"Four!"

With sickening realization Tufton saw that May did not intend to intervene. Should the young deputy aim to go through with his threat, it offered a solution to his problem. A bullet in the head would prevent Tufton making incriminating statements. So May kept quiet and none of his men made a move to help the promoter. Seeing that he stood alone, Tufton let out a hoarse screech of terror and followed on the boxer's heels at, if possible, greater speed.

"This's all your doing!" Taffy hissed, swinging to face Ginger. "I'm go—"

"Through that door right now!" put in a grim female voice and Fran shoved through the crowd and then between the two girls. "If you don't go, I'm going to take you apart— And I'll be ready for any dirty game like you pulled tonight."

During the time they had traveled together, Taffy had been matched regularly against the older woman. While she often won, she knew that the results had always been pre-arranged. Only the unexpected trick that evening had given her victory. If she tangled with Fran again, it would not be in a trained routine and she knew success would be anything but assured. Nor did Taffy fancy facing the obviously furious Fran right then.

So, to the disappointment of the watching crowd, Taffy slunk out of the room and Fran followed her.

"All right, gents," May announced. "That's all—"

"You're wrong, Mr. May," Waco interrupted. "That's not all. There's something you forgot."

"What?" growled the theater owner.

"You offered two hundred and fifty dollars to the winner."

"Two hu— That was for the prize-fight, not for running a yeller-bellied pack out of the room."

"May," Waco said in a cold, contemptuous voice. "You've got the heart of a stinking, four-flushing mac from a hog-ranch. All right, keep your money, but I'm having one turn of the wheel."

"Tur—!" May began in a puzzled voice.

"On that fancy roulette wheel. Just one to get that two hundred and fifty dollars you're gypping me out of."

"Are you backing him, Counter?" May demanded.

"Every last inch of the way," Mark agreed.

"One spin?"

"That's all I need," Waco assured him. "Loan me two hundred and fifty bucks, will you, Mark?"

"It's all yours," the blond giant answered, taking out his wallet.

Watched by the silent crowd, May, the Texans and Ginger went to the roulette table. After May saw Waco drop the money on the table, he spun the wheel and reached towards the ball.

"We don't need that for this spin, mister," Waco stated, right hand hovering with spread fingers over the Colt's butt.

"How's that?" May demanded.

"You hired Ginger because she was broke and some stinking thief back East got her to sign a paper for enough money to come out here. If she quits working for you, or gets fired, you don't send the money to that son-of-a-bitch in Philadelphia and he tells fellers out here to work her over good."

"If she told you tha—!" the theater owner started.

"You're calling a lady, and a friend of *mine* a liar, *hombre!*" Waco warned.

"So I paid her debts for her. She could work it off here."

"How long'd it take? Two hundred and fifty dollars, and the interest out of her pay, with some of it took off her each time for one reason or another. How long, May. One year, two, more?"

"I've been here five years and still ain't clear!" yelled a woman's voice from among the crowd.

"In three years I've not got mine down more than a hundred simoleons!" another went on.

"The wheel's slowing, May," Waco said. "I'm telling you that I've won."

There the theater owner had it placed before him as plain as he could wish. He could refuse to accept that statement, but only by implying that Waco lied. To do so under the present conditions would bring only one answer. If he wished to make the accusation, he must back it with a gun—and he knew just how little chance he stood against that soft-spoken boy who should have been his dupe.

"Y-you win," May confirmed. "And I'll see—"

"You'll see nobody," Waco corrected. "Right now I'm going to talk to those fist-fighters and I reckon they're scared enough to give me true answers. If I find that you're trying to set me up with them, I'll be looking for you. Mister, whether they say anything or not, comes morning I'll be around— And I'll spit in your face every time we meet."

"Anybody who takes sides faces me and the rest of the floating outfit," Mark went on. "It's your choice, all of you."

Nobody spoke as a scowling May paid over the money, nor offered to interfere. Putting the money into his pocket, Waco handed Mark's loan back to its owner. Then he grinned at Ginger and offered her his arm.

"Come on, Ginger gal," he said. "You've just worked off all you owed."

With that the youngster escorted the girl from the building and Mark followed at a more leisurely pace, watching the crowd. After the doors closed, May let out a long sigh. If he never came closer to death, he would feel contented. Yet the affair might be saved even at that late hour.

"Drinks on the house, gents!" he announced, usually a good way of regaining favor.

Only for once nobody moved. While his employees studied him with blank indifference, he read open hostility on the faces of the customers. Spitting on to the floor, the buffalo hunter collected his gun and looked May over from head to toe.

"I'm a mite choosey who I takes even free drinks off," the hunter declared. "Which same, I wouldn't touch one from you was I dying of thirst."

"That goes for me" a cowhand went on. "Let's go, boys."

Fury filled May as he watched the men filing out of the room. Looking at his employees, he saw no sign that they intended to back him. So he must face the wrath of the

Texans alone, for he knew that Tufton would talk. That meant only one course remained open to him. Turning, he hurried to his office with the intention of gathering the means to leave town and start up in a safer location.

"They've gone, deputy," Fran told Mark when he, Waco and Ginger went to the hotel in search of Tufton. "Took two of the horses, all the money and run out on us."

"The lousy, stinking bums, both of them," Taffy sniffed, eyeing the grim-faced Texans. "They've left us stranded here—and after all I did for them."

"Just what did you do for them?" Waco demanded.

"I helped rig that trouble tonight—"

"Why you—!" Ginger yelped, moving towards the blonde.

"Hold her there, hot-head," grinned Mark, catching Ginger under the arms and lifting her from the ground without apparent effort. "Leave her talk."

"Tufton and May'd rigged it just like you said, handsome," Taffy told Waco. "All I did was what they made me do."

"Show the deputies the bruises they made hitting you with money, Taffy," Fran suggested dryly. "What're you going to do with us, mister?"

"You, ma'am," Mark replied, setting Ginger down and smiling at the older woman. "Way I see it, you weren't sat in on the game. And I don't reckon your pard did more than she had to."

"What'll happen to us now Sid's run out, Fran?" Taffy whined.

"I'd say you're fine," Waco put in.

"But they took all the money and two horses—" the blonde protested.

"And left you a good wagon, that fancy fist-fighting stage and all the other gear," Waco pointed out.

"Hey, yes," Fran ejaculated. "I'd forgot that. Ben's going to live. It'll be a fair spell before he can go in the ring, but he can train some kid we pick up. You and me can keep the show going until he does, Taffy."

"You mean you'd take me along after tonight?" Taffy gasped.

"Why not. You've got faults, but it'll be quicker than training up a new gal."

"Could you train one?" Ginger asked eagerly.

"Sure. If she's willing to learn."

"You?" Taffy inquired, eyeing Ginger with surprise.

"Me!" the little redhead replied, glaring in a "Want to make something of it" manner at the blonde.

"It's a hard life," Fran warned.

"Sister," Ginger answered. "You should see the way I've been living for the past months."

"How about it, Taffy?" the brunette asked. "Do we take her along?"

"Why not?" Taffy answered. "If she can stand the pace, and I reckon she can, another girl'll be just what we need."

Waco and Ginger walked along the street towards the marshal's office, with Mark following them.

"Why'd you do that, Ginger gal?" the youngster demanded. "You've the money to clear yourself with that jasper. You could've gone back to Mulrooney."

"As a failure," she answered. "If I can make it with Fran, at least I'll not be that."

"You'll make it," Mark prophesied. "What we'll do is send the money to a Philadelphia lawyer and let him pay off that jasper. That way we'll make certain he can't say it never came. You'll be all right, Ginger gal."

"Only you're still going to spend the night where we can watch out for you," Waco went on. "After you're at the office, Mark, me and a couple of the boys're going back to make talk with May."

Ginger chuckled. "From the look on his face when you told him you'd be coming to see him, you'll have a walk for nothing."

And the girl proved to be correct. After leaving her in

Doc's care, Waco, Mark, Dusty and the Kid returned to the theater. They found it empty of customers and with its owner's office showing signs of a hurried departure which reminded them of when they went to see Bellamy. Another source of evil had left Trail End, making one more step in the work of cleaning up the town.

PART FIVE

Coulton's Try

Nobody could say that the fight going on in the Golden Nugget Saloon—one of the smaller places in Trail End—lacked spirit or fair play. Considering that two rival trail crews formed the bulk of the fighters, everything went on without serious blood-shedding. True an occasional chair or bottle might be used as a club, or a boot sank into ribs, but firearms remained in holsters. So neither the owner nor the two deputies saw any point in intervening until things quietened down a mite.

Leaning on the wall, Mark Counter and Doc Leroy looked through the batwing doors. Nor did Erasmus O'Hagen seem perturbed at the thought that some of his portable property might be damaged. One of the more honest saloonkeepers, O'Hagen could never compete with the flashier, more opulent places like the May Day Music Hall, First Chance, Blazing Pine or others in the town's center. Since the closure of several such places, his own business had boomed and he possessed good enough sense to know the increase in trade meant higher overheads. For the volume of custom garnered, he knew he must accept the occasional brawl. Not that he expected to come out a loser, for the participants would pay for any damage caused and some more.

"Sure and tis good to see the boyos enjoying themselves," O'Hagen said. "And a broth of a fight it is at that."

"You should see the OD Connected and Double B when they get started," Doc told him, showing a cowhand's typical loyalty to the brand he worked for. "Hell, we do this good in the middle of the month."

"Not every month," Mark objected. "Only one in thr—"

To the tune of crashing glass a cowhand pitched through the left side window and interrupted the blond giant's comments. Rising, the man let out an angry bellow and started to draw his gun. Instantly the relaxation fell from Mark. Springing along the sidewalk, he shot out a big hand to clamp hold of the revolver and twist it from the other's grasp. With an exclamation of fury, the cowhand spun to face his unexpected assailant. His eyes focused on Mark's chest and ranged upwards, comparing his own five foot nine with the height and heft of the blond giant.

"Damn it," he said with a drunken gravity after completing his examination. "If there warn't two of you one sat a-top the other, I'd whup you good for that."

"I'll bet there's some little fellers inside," Mark replied.

"By cracky, yes!" agreed the cowhand, pleased with such a solution to his problem. "And I'll chaw their ears off outa meanness when I get back."

With that he bounded through the window and came backwards from it almost immediately, landing on the sidewalk in a glassy-eyed pile. Mark grinned and walked back to his companions.

"Won't he have a head comes morning," the blond giant said. "I'll bet he swears off drinking through it."

"If cowhands kept to that, I'd be out of business and so'd every other saloonkeeper in the West," O'Hagen answered.

Deftly Doc halted the rearwards rush of a man who burst through the batwing doors. Ducking under a wild punch launched by the ungrateful fighter, Doc shoved him back into the room.

"Reckon we ought to stop them, Mark?" Doc inquired.

"Devil the bit," O'Hagen replied before the other could speak. "Hell, I've not had a good fight in my place since those flash traps along the street opened. There's plenty of furniture to be had cheap around town and those boys'll pay for the damage they do."

None of the trio noticed a tall, lean young man approaching at a run. He wore a derby hat on lank, untidy black hair, and was dressed in a rumpled town suit of good quality, a grubby white shirt and red tie. Sallow complexioned, his gaunt face held an expression of arrogant, condescending superiority. In his left hand he held a notebook and the right gripped a pencil.

"What's going on here?" the newcomer demanded, skidding to a halt.

Turning, Doc studied the speaker from head to toe. "I'd say a fight's going on, mister. Wouldn't you, Mark?"

Two struggling men barged through the doors. Catching them by their collars, Mark heaved them back inside before replying to his *amigo*'s question.

"Yeah, Doc. I reckon you called it right. There *is* a fight going on."

"And you're standing out here, doing nothing?" yelped the new arrival.

"It's a private fight, mister," Mark answered. "We've not been invited."

"But you're peace officers—!"

"And it's sure peaceful—" Mark told him, pausing to heave a cursing townsman back through the doors when the latter charged out with bloody nose and torn jacket. "Out here."

"You should stop them!" the young man stated.

"Why?"

"That's what the Governor brought you in for. To stop trail drive crews rampaging through the town."

"You show us where they're rampaging through and we'll stop them," Mark promised. "Mostly, though, we were brought in to bust out as mean a pack of shysters, four-flushers and back-shooting thieves as ever preyed on folks who come to a trail end town."

"I see," purred the young man, slashing down notes in shorthand on the open book. Then he looked at O'Hagen. "Are you the owner?"

"That I am."

"And you are satisfied with the way these deputies are acting?"

"Ain't seed one of 'em spit on the sidewalk all evening. Just who might you be, if you don't mind the question?"

"My name is Proudman, Eustace Proudman," the young man replied in a tone that suggested no more need be said. He made the next words seem almost like an afterthought, unnecessary in more cultural company. "I'm a reporter for the *Kansas City Intelligencer*."

Doc and Mark exchanged glances, for they knew what kind of newspaper Proudman represented. Run by the Radical Republican element, the *Kansas City Intelligencer* acted on behalf of the "underdog", which meant anybody in opposition to authority. By far the loudest objections to the floating outfit's appointment had come from the *Intelligencer*. Ever since arriving in Trail End, Dusty and Mark had expected the paper to send along a reporter. Proudman could hardly have come at a less opportune moment.

"Reckon the boys've had enough for one night, Raz?" Mark inquired.

"Sure, I reckon they have," the saloonkeeper answered, eyeing Proudman in a manner hardly complimentary to such a stout defender of the "people's" rights. "Will you be needing any help?"

"Nope. Just go get set to start doing business again," Mark replied and walked through the doors. Looking around, he saw that the fighters showed signs of exhaustion and figured they would welcome an excuse to give up as long as it could be done without loss of face. Drawing his right hand Colt, he fired a shot into the roof at the far corner of the room. "Simmer down, you cow-prodding yahoos! You've had your fun. Now let the boss start earning some money."

Shot and bellow combined to bring the fighting to a halt. Before anybody could think of resuming hostilities, O'-Hagen walked in with a yelled offer of drinks on the house. That clinched the bid for peace. Already the rival crews figured they had asserted their superiority over the other side and looked for a way to get back to their celebrations. Those of the cowhands who remembered Mark from Mulrooney figured obedience to be less painful than the consequences of refusal; and the chance of a free drink sealed their resolve. Separating from their opponents, the men headed for the bar. O'Hagen's bartender appeared from the backroom to which he had retired with the girls when the fight started. Once the flow of free drinks commenced, the girls came back and mingled with the customers.

Picking up a discarded hat, Mark placed it on the bar. "All right now," he announced. "Dip in. The damage's got to be paid for."

"Shucks, us Walking Y boys allus pay for our fun, Mark," replied the segundo of that outfit and his companions gave their agreement.

"The Flying D'll match anything you put up," snorted the leader of that faction, just as Mark knew he would.

At the door Proudman watched with annoyance as the customers trooped along the bar to feed donations into the hat. In addition to the free-handed generosity of cowhands, neither trail crew wished to let the other out-do it. So they paid up eagerly, willingly and with such good spirit that O'Hagen later found he could replace all the damaged or destroyed property and still show a profit.

Not that Proudman would have wanted to hear that. His kind only sought to establish true facts when those facts suited their purpose. Seeing there would be no chance of gaining anything his paper wanted, he turned and made his way to the Good Fortune gambling house. There he requested an interview with the owner.

"I see why you sent word for the paper to send a man, Mr. Coulton," the reporter said. "There was a fight at the Golden Nugget and two deputies just stood watching it. If I hadn't arrived, they wouldn't've made a move to stop it."

"That's what I told your boss," Coulton answered, glancing uneasily around the room. "All those damned Texans do is abuse honest businessmen. They let the trail crews run wild."

"I'll get my story off right away," Proudman promised.

"Yeah, you do that," Coulton replied.

All in all, the saloonkeeper would have preferred that the reporter had done so without visiting him. While Coulton had sent to the editor of the *Intelligencer,* he did not wish his connection with the paper known.

"It would've been a better story if the owner of the Golden Nugget had wanted the deputies to end the fight and they refused," Proudman remarked frankly. "But he seemed happy enough with the way they handled it."

"Maybe he didn't dare do anything but act like he was," Coulton suggested.

"How do you mean?" asked the reporter eagerly.

"Those Texans've closed three places since they came.

Any saloonkeeper who doesn't go along with them's soon out of business."

"Maybe I should see him again when they're not around."

"Sure," Coulton agreed, then a thought struck him and he went on. "Only if I was you, I'd leave him until tomorrow."

"Why?"

"He'll be free to speak then. Right now I bet those damned rebs are watching him. Them or some of their kind."

"It might be best," Proudman breathed. "Yes, that's what I'll do, leave it until tomorrow."

"And another thing," the saloonkeeper remarked as Proudman turned to leave. "Don't come around here too often. I like your company, but if those Texans knew I'd sent for you, they'd make things real awkward for me."

Being vicious and small-minded enough to act in such a manner, Proudman assumed everybody would do the same. So he accepted Coulton's explanation and hastened to reassure the other.

"I understand and I'll make sure that our readers learn the true conditions in Trail End."

"If I reckoned you'd do that," Coulton thought, watching the reporter walk towards the doors, "I'd kill you where you stand."

If nothing else, Coulton was honest with himself.

Passing through the front doors of the Good Fortune, Proudman almost bumped into Mark and Doc as they were returning to the office from the Golden Nugget. He spun on his heel and hurried away, crossing the street without a backwards glance. Although a fearless exposer of "social evils", he only did so when sure there could be no painful repercussions against him.

"What do you reckon he wanted in the Good Fortune, Mark?" Doc asked.

"Maybe he went looking for another fight we've not stopped," the blond giant replied. "Lord, Doc, I can never look at one of that sort without wanting to squash it under my boot."

"If they ever find a way to pass out their ideas to ordinary folks, not just a few who read their stinking papers, the world'll be a sorry place," Doc commented. "Maybe we'd best go tell Dusty that the *Intelligencer*'s come to town."

By the time Mark and Doc reached the office, Dusty already knew of Proudman's presence in town. Walking into the marshal's building, the deputies found Mayor Galt already there. While the mayor made no further attempts to impede their work, he remained constantly in the background. Keeping his finger delicately on the pulse of public opinion, Galt watched and waited. He felt the pinch, due to the Texans' activities, for his major sources of income no longer existed. After his inability to prevent the gambling-inspection ordinance, the various contributions to his "campaign funds" had ceased. Nor, in view of Dusty's ideas on the matter, could he claim donations from the brothels in return for ensuring that the local law did not interfere with their running.

The only times Mayor Galt visited the marshal's office were when he came to lodge a complaint, or brought word of potential trouble.

"The situation is very delicate, Captain Fog," Mark and Doc heard Galt saying as they entered.

"It's been that way since we came," Dusty replied. "Why the sudden rush to warn us about it?"

"I've just heard that a reporter form the *Intelligencer*'s in town."

"So?"

"You know the kind of paper it is?"

"I've a real good idea."

"It commands a large following in Kansas and they accept everything it prints as correct."

"Some folks'd believe in fairies and Father Christmas," Mark put in dryly.

"The thing is that not even the Governor can flout the *Intelligencer*'s opinions with impunity," Galt went on, ignoring the comment.

"I don't reckon Governor Mansfield scares that easy," Dusty remarked. "I know his brother down in Arizona Territory doesn't.* Anyways, what's this got to do with us?"

"The Governor appointed you, Captain Fog, against strong opposition at all levels of society in the State. So your conduct here reflects on him."

"Just what's been wrong with our conduct so far, Mayor?" Doc demanded.

"Nothing!" Galt hastened to reply. "Well, there're some who might say that you've been too severe in some cases—"

"Such as?" Dusty asked.

"I don't want to state any particular instance, not knowing all the facts," Galt answered, his politician's instincts steering him from any direct comment that he might later be called upon to confirm or deny. "From the little I've heard, you seem justified in closing all those places. But you've made enemies doing it."

"And a few friends, maybe?"

"I'm not gainsaying it, Captain, some folks say that you've cleaned out a lot of the town's worst elements. But others claim your methods are too heavy-handed."

"Any man who throws down on me or my deputies'll be stopped, Mayor," Dusty stated. "Just as fast as we can stop him."

"Nobody objects to your men defending themselves," Galt replied. "But— Well, two days ago I saw Mr. Counter

*Dusty's connection with the Governor of Arizona is told in *Wagons to Backsight*.

bang two men's heads together, knock them unconscious and drag them to the jail by their collars."

"They were a couple of gandy-dancers, hawg-wild drunk and fighting in the street," Mark said. "When they're like that the best time to tell them to stop fighting's after you've made sure they can't do anything but stop."

Galt could not deny that the men in question had been fighting and causing inconvenience to the other users of the street. So he sought for another example.

"How about that cowhand you threw out of the Bella Union the day before?"

"He figured he should shoot up the fixings and I didn't, so I tossed him for it," Mark replied. "Must've tossed him a mite too hard."

"This's no joking matter, Mr. Counter," the mayor observed severely.

"Nothing to do with guns is," Mark answered. "And when I go after some yahoo fooling around with one, I don't go gentle."

"But those are the kind of incidents this feller'll be looking for," Galt warned. "Exposing the so-called brutalities by peace officers's always been a prime game of the *Intelligencer*."

"I can't remember them ever exposing the Earps for busting trail hands' heads in Dodge," Dusty commented. "Or raising any sweat over the way Jackley used to treat our boys here in Trail End."

Even Galt could not deny that. Being a paper run by liberal-intellectuals, the *Intelligencer* selected the kind of "underdogs" it protected. Texans, by their support of the Confederate States in the War—thereby having the effrontery to go against the liberal-intellectuals' theories of how the world should be—did not deserve the protection given to such worthy "underdogs" as murderers, thieves, rabble-rousers and idle, work-shy bums.

Being a professional politician, Galt neither denied nor confirmed Dusty's statement. Instead he coughed and turned his attention to the small Texan.

"You see what I mean, Captain Fog?"

"I see, Mayor. And I'll warn my deputies to watch their step. But we'll do anything that needs doing, any way we have to, and to hell with the *Intelligencer*."

"That's all I ask," Galt replied and, clearly satisfied that he had performed his civic duty, walked from the office.

"Don't forget, Mark, Doc," Dusty told his deputies after the front door had closed. "Walk soft and gentle if that *Intelligencer* yahoo's around."

"I never thought you'd let some stinking soft-shell son-of-a-bitch worry you, Dusty," Doc growled.

"He doesn't worry me for myself. When we're done here, no matter which way it goes, we'll be headed for home. Governor Mansfield'll be left in Kansas. And, Doc, don't you forget that he's the straightest man you're likely to see in office up here. Get somebody the *Intelligencer* goes for as governor and this State'll be hell on earth for us Texans."

"You're right," Doc admitted. "Like always."

"That's what I like, loyal, respectful hired help," Dusty grinned, then became sober. "Remember, walk easy. Don't do anything he could call abusing folks if he's around. But don't get yourselves killed either."

"If I have to shoot anybody, I'll let him put a couple of bullets into me first," Mark promised. "Then Proudman'll know I acted in self-defense."

"You do that," Dusty grinned. "Now how about going out and earning your pay?"

After Dusty, Mark topped Proudman's list to be "exposed" by the *Intelligencer*. In addition to his prominence as a member of the floating outfit, the blond giant possessed other qualities guaranteed to rouse the reporter's hatred. Being a rich Southerner alone would have turned Proudman against him. That he also was very handsome, with a splendid physique, and competent, increased the reporter's envy. With Proudman's kind, to envy was to hate and, if it could be done without risk, to destroy the one better favored.

So Proudman decided that Mark would be his first target. With that thought in mind, he followed as Mark walked from the Elite Plaza Hotel to the marshal's office on the morning after the fight. Aware of the other's presence, Mark hoped nothing would happen. Fate appeared to be working against the blond giant, for he came across something that could have been easily handled under other circumstances.

Seated on the bench outside the Wells Fargo office, Darby Clegg elevated his feet to the hitching rail and caused all other users of the sidewalk to take to the street. Almost as tall as Mark, heavily built and bearded, Clegg wore range clothes and belted a low-hanging Colt. To folks lacking knowledge of the West, he looked like a cowhand. Mark doubted if Clegg had ever ridden for any brand and figured he belonged to a class of drifter all too common in Trail End and other such towns. Working as little as possible, skirting on the fringes of actual outlawry, men like Clegg lived on the bounty of others, joined in any fun going as long as their part in it be free, or could be found involved by any trouble that came.

A tall, sturdy youngster of no more than fourteen years stood admiringly at Clegg's side. Dressed in good clothes, he came from a respectable family in the upper middle-income bracket, or Mark read the signs wrong.

"Yes, sir, Jimmy boy," Clegg was saying, ignoring the sight of a woman toting a shopping basket having to detour around him, "all the owlhoots know Darby Clegg. Why I've rid with most of the best at one time and another."

"You're blocking the sidewalk, mister," Mark said, halting.

"So?" Clegg demanded, looking up but not moving.

"So how about setting down your feet and letting folks get by?"

"Them and you c'n walk 'round!"

"Is th—," Mark began. Then he remembered Proudman and stopped both his words and proposed course of action.

At Mark's cold comment and pace forward, Clegg brought down his feet ready to rise. Then he saw the hesitation and remembered hearing of Proudman being in town. Like most of his kind, Clegg knew the *Intelligencer*'s editorial policy; especially how it affected the likes of him when in conflict with a peace officer. Guessing that Mark would avoid trouble of a kind that might be mis-called brawling in the street, Clegg pushed the issue farther than he would have dared at any other time. Rising to his feet, he grinned with cocky assurance at the blond giant.

"You reckon you can make me shift?"

"It looks like I just did," Mark answered and walked by.

Young Jimmy Griddle stood watching Mark's departure with mixed emotions. Up to that time he had always regarded the Texas peace officers as tough, unafraid men who could not be insulted with impunity. So he thought to see Mark take much stronger action than merely tricking Darby Clegg into standing up.

"You sure made Mark Counter back water, Darby," the youngster said, with a trace of disappointment in his voice.

"Hah!" Clegg snorted. "All lawmen are yeller. Come on, let's go see what's doing around town."

With that Clegg swung around and started to walk off in the opposite direction to that taken by Mark. A disappointed Proudman thrust his notebook away as the man and boy approached him. Wondering if he should make an issue of Mark not taking stronger action against Clegg for blocking the path, as there could be no accusation of abusing a peaceable citizen, the reporter felt himself thrust aside. Grinning at Jimmy, Clegg staggered Proudman out of his path and continued walking.

"You're sure tough, Darby," Jimmy said as they turned down an alley between two buildings. "I bet nobody'd stand up to you."

"There's not many who dare, and none twice," Clegg answered. "Say, how'd you like to meet some for-real owlhoots?"

"Boy! Wouldn't I just?" Jimmy enthused. "Can you take me to meet 'em?"

At another time, knowing his exact standing in outlaw circles, Clegg would never have made such a suggestion. However he saw a way out of future trouble. The fact that he had got away with his behavior to Mark Counter did not fool him. Only the knowledge that the *Intelligencer* had a man looking and hoping for some such incident had saved Clegg from the treatment his conduct deserved. On their next meeting the big blond might not have such an inducement to stay passive.

Leaving town became a prime necessity, which brought up a major point: how to do it. Bucking the tiger at the Good Fortune had cleaned him out, while his horse and saddle had long since gone as a means of obtaining cash. So he must find some way of making his departure. Riding the box-cars of the railroad was too risky and he did not care to work his way on a freight outfit, always assuming he could find one willing to hire him.

Clegg thanked the good sense which had made him cultivate Jimmy. Among the other things he had learned was that the youngster's father owned a pair of fast saddle-horses. With a little thought, Clegg felt that he could gain possession of them.

"'Course, leaving's going to need thinking on," he said. "We can't just haul up and walk out of here."

"What'd we want so as to leave?" Jimmy asked.

"Food, money, hosses."

"I can get food and my paw's got a pair of good hosses we can use."

"He'll never let us borrow them."

"Shucks, he's out of town from noon so he'll not know. Only I've no money."

"That's my side of it, pardner," Clegg grinned, delighted in the way the boy was playing into his hands. "You don't like ole Pop Ericks, do you?"

"Naw. He's a mean ole goat," Jimmy replied. "He whupped me for taking some apples off his trees."

"Then we'll take his store afore we leave," Clegg promised. "Money, enough food and all the rest we need. And a gun-rig and Colt for you if you want."

"That'll be swell!" Jimmy enthused. "And it'll serve him right."

"When's your pappy leaving town?"

"On the noon train."

"All right, bring the hosses, saddled up ready, to Ericks' store around one o'clock and we'll be riding out before half after."

"You're the boss, Darby," Jimmy breathed excitedly.

"And remember, not a word to anybody about this," the man warned as the boy turned to dart away.

"Coulton's up to something, Cap'n Fog," Mousey said, standing before the desk in the marshal's office. "He's got Will Otley and two more hard-cases around there this morning and's still with 'em."

"I thought Coulton'd been quiet," Dusty remarked, half to himself. "Any idea what's doing?"

"Only that it's something to do with that *Intelligencer* feller being in town," the little informer answered. "Maybe Coulton wants to show him that you and your boys can't run the town."

"Could be," Dusty agreed, sliding the usual payment across the desk top and watching it disappear. "When're you going to tell me who's collecting the hog-ranches take, Mousey?"

"I've tried to learn, Cap'n," the other answered, glancing nervously at the office door as it opened, then relaxing as Mark entered. "If I'd more to spend—"

"Not having enough to spend's the cause of half the

world's troubles," Dusty smiled. "Thanks for the word."

"You're welcome," the little informer replied and left by the side entrance.

"What's up, Mark?" Dusty inquired, seeing the anger on the blond giant's face. "You looked riled."

"That stinking soft-shell—" Mark began hotly, then launched into a profane description of the incident in the street. "Damn it," he concluded. "If he hadn't been there, I'd've tossed that big-mouthed yack half way across the street. Now a fool kid reckons I'm yeller and that the jasper he was with's a real tough *hombre*. If that soft-shell keeps dogging me—"

"That's just what I want him to do," Dusty interrupted.

"What!"

"While he's after you, he can't be watching the other boys," the small Texan explained. "And that could be mighty important, Mark."

"How come?"

"Mousey's just brought word. He reckons Coulton's planning something."

"We've expected it," Mark stated.

"Sure. But Coulton's smarter than those yahoos we've bust out of town. It was him who brought that reporter in."

"I wondered what took that stinking soft-shell into the Good Fortune last night," Mark breathed. "He looked a mite put out to see me and Doc as he came out."

"That was after the fight ended," Dusty replied, thinking back to what Mark had told him and looking towards the door as the rest of the floating outfit came in.

"Sure," agreed Mark. "And that jasper didn't go a whole heap on how we handled it. If Raz O'Hagen hadn't backed us up—"

"Yeah," Dusty put in. "If Raz hadn't backed you, there'd've been one hell of a story for the *Intelligencer*."

"But he backed us," Doc commented.

"What if he changes his story?"

"Hell, Dusty. Raz wouldn't do that," Mark objected. "He's one of the straightest fellers in town."

"He's real straight, for a Republican," the Kid remarked.

Once again Waco showed the flair for deduction soon to make him such a valuable asset in Captain Bertram Mosehan's fight to clean up Arizona Territory.*

"Only something could happen to make him change his mind," the youngster guessed. "He doesn't look like a feller who'd scare easy, but he's got a wife and right pretty lil daughter."

"You've hit it, boy," Dusty said. "Mark, I want you to keep that *Intelligencer* yahoo busy, so's the rest of us can do what we have to do."

"Where's your boss?" Will Otley demanded of the old swamper engaged in cleaning up the results of the fight and a subsequent roaring evening's business.

"Ye'll have to speak up a mite, son," the swamper answered, cupping a hand around his off ear. "I'm a mite deef."

"Looking for me, friend?" O'Hagen called from the door of his office.

"If you're the boss," agreed Otley.

"I'm not hiring any dealers," the saloonkeeper stated, studying the other's elegant professional gambler style of dress and low hanging Colt. "Don't need any."

"Maybe you don't know just what you do need," Otley purred. "Let's talk."

"Come on in here and do it private," offered O'Hagen.

On entering the office, Otley looked around him with a wary alertness. He saw only the usual fittings, desk, couple of chairs, safe—although the large wardrobe at the side of the room might be an item not normally found in the boss's

*Told in *Sagebrush Sleuth, Arizona Ranger, Waco Rides In*.

private place of business.

"Hear you had some trouble last night," the hard-case commented, crossing the room and sitting on the edge of the desk.

"Nothing to worry over."

"The law didn't stop it, though."

"You heard wrong, feller. Those two deputies handled things just right."

"That's not what I heard," Otley insisted. "Fact being, a whole heap of folks say they ought to've moved sooner to stop it."

"Somebody'd've got hurt bad if they'd tried," O'Hagen answered.

"That's not what folks say."

"That's what I say!"

"Maybe you ought to change your mind," Otley said quietly. "Yes sir. I'd reckon you should oughta change your mind. Like if anybody comes 'round asking, you should say you asked them deputies to stop it and they wouldn't."

"That'd be a lie."

"You've got a real pretty wife and lil gal, O'Hagen. You wouldn't want anything to happen to them, now would you?"

"Nothing'd better happen to 'em," O'Hagen growled. "So what's this about?"

"Only if the feller from the *Intelligencer* don't hear—"

The words trailed off as some instinct screamed its warning to Otley. Suspicious by nature, training and employment, he remained constantly alert for traps. Suddenly he realized that the saloonkeeper was taking the whole affair far too calmly. Instead of showing concern, fear or anger over the threat to his family, O'Hagen gave the appearance of expecting the visit. Maybe even had help on hand.

There was only one place in the room where a man could hide. Dropping from the edge of the desk, Otley turned his eyes to the wardrobe and his hand flashed to the holstered gun.

Instantly the wardrobe door flew open and Waco burst from his place inside. Although the youngster had hoped to remain concealed until learning Otley's full intentions, he saw there would be no chance. Watching the interview through one of the decorative holes in the door, he examined Otley and reached a similar conclusion from O'Hagen's actions. Only Waco reached it a short time before the hard-case. So when the youngster made his appearance, he came with a gun in each hand and full ready for trouble.

Flame tore from two guns, the concussion of exploding powder reverberating through the room. Waco heard lead pass over his head and knew the bullet from his right hand Colt had found a billet in the wall without striking its target. Seeing that he had also missed, Otley started to cock his Colt on its recoil. The hard-case worked with the swift, deadly precision of one well-versed in such matters. Only Waco did not need to take the time to draw back the hammer of his fired Colt. In his other hand he held a weapon ready for use. Before Otley could complete the thumbing back of the hammer, Waco fired his left hand gun. Slamming into Otley's chest, the bullet sent him stumbling backwards. He hit the wall, fingers opening to let the gun fall. Then he slipped down to the floor, limp and coughing away his life-blood.

"Damn it!" Waco growled, walking across the room to kick Otley's gun aside. "Dusty wanted him able to talk."

"It was him or you, young feller and me next if he dropped you," O'Hagen replied. "There wasn't anything else you could've done agin a feller like him."

"I reckon not," Waco agreed. "It was just like Dusty figured. They aimed to make you lie about us."

"That they did. Now I only hope that Cap'n Fog's right about them guarding my wife and kid."

"You can count on it," the youngster promised.

At that moment a man was forcing his way by O'Hagen's plump, normally cheery-faced wife into the saloonkeeper's house.

"Keep quiet and you won't get hurt, missus," he told her.

"That's just what I was going to say to you," put in a male voice and Doc Leroy stepped out of the sitting-room behind his cocked, lined Colt.

Letting out a low hiss, the man reached towards Mrs. O'Hagen with the intention of using her as a shield. Before Doc could take any action, the woman showed herself far from being a meek, defenseless female. Alerted for the possibility of such an attempt, she had insisted on continuing with her housework and answered the door carrying a sweeping broom in one hand. Swiftly she took hold of it with her other hand, driving the end of the handle straight up under the man's jaw. Pain and the force of the impact rocked him backwards, hands jerking away from his proposed protection. Nor had Mrs. O'Hagen finished with him. Defty she lowered the broom's handle to thrust it into the pit of his stomach. Unable to retreat, he let out a croak of agony and doubled over. Up, around then down swung the broom, its head colliding with the man and tumbling him to the ground.

"Take that, yez spalpeen!" Mrs. O'Hagen yelled. "I'll teach yez to come threatening a poor defenseless woman in her home."

"Leave some of him for us, ma'am," Doc grinned, walking forward.

"That I will," she replied. "'Tis a sorry day when the likes of him can come scaring decent womenfolk."

"I reckon he'd give you an argument about who's scared," Doc chuckled, jerking the revolver from the unresisting man's holster. "Likely he'll want to tell us why he come here."

"To bring a message," the man muttered, sitting against the wall and rubbing his aching skull.

"Who sent you?"

"You'd best call this beef-head off, missus," the man

growled, ignoring Doc's question. "Or your daughter'll wish you had."

"*Hombre!*" the slim Texan put in. "Do you know what amputation means?"

"Sure I do. When a doctor cuts a feller's arm or leg off 'cause it's hurt."

"And that's just what I'm going to do to you if anything happens to the girl. Only your leg and arm won't be hurt—until I get started."

Looking at Doc's cold, grim expression, the man shuddered and did not doubt the threat would be carried out.

"It's nothing to do with me!" he wailed. "I'm only following orders. One of the other fellers's gone to grab the gal out of school. Honest, deputy, I don't know anything about it."

"Then you'd best start praying that the girl's all right," Doc replied.

At the school, a tall, unshaven hard-case looked at the impressive form of Miss Andrews for a moment before making his request. "Mrs. O'Hagen sent me to fetch her daughter home," he said.

"I'll tell her," the teacher promised, turning and walking into the building without giving him a chance to carry on with the story fabricated by Coulton.

Before the man could think about the remarkable ease with which Miss Andrews had accepted his story, a whistle sounded from inside the schoolhouse. Hooves thudded and he turned to see a magnificent white stallion swing into view around the corner. Big, wild-looking, the horse appeared as dangerous as a grizzly bear met on a narrow ledge.

"The gal don't want to come, *hombre,*" said a voice from the doorway. "So you'll have to make do with lil ole me."

At the first word the man started to turn, hand fanning downwards. Only he never completed the move. Standing at the door, black-dressed and menacing as a Comanche hunting for the white-eye brother's scalp, the Ysabel Kid looked him over with mocking eyes. Held with negligent competence, the Winchester possessed more threat than a battery of Napoleon cannon. Halting his hand's movement, the man tried to assume an air of innocence.

"What's up, deputy?" he asked.

"I was hoping you'd tell me that," the Kid replied. "After you've let your gunbelt drop."

"Shucks," the hard-case answered, unbuckling his belt and allowing it to slide away. "Mrs. O'Hagen asked me to come fetch her lil gal home from school and I done it out-a the goodness of my heart."

"Why sure," agreed the Kid, bending to gather up the discarded belt. "And I'm the President of the Confederate States of America." With that he stepped back into the school where Miss Andrews was waiting. "I don't reckon there'll be any more of 'em, ma'am. But if anybody should come around—"

"I'll know what to do," the schoolteacher answered grimly. "Won't that man escape while you're talking to me?"

"If he does, he'll not get far, ma'am," the Kid assured her. "Thanks for the help."

Leaving the building, the Kid found the hard-case waiting. Not that he expected otherwise, with the white stallion standing guard.

"What now?" asked the man with more bluster than he felt.

"We're going to the O'Hagen house," the Kid explained. "Should it come out I'm wronging you, I'll apologize most humble. But if Mrs. O'Hagen didn't send you for her lil gal— Waal, you 'n' me's going to have us a lil talk to learn who did."

Fear bit into the hard-case as he stared at the Kid's face and read what the soft-spoken words meant.

"Th-there's a feller from the *Intelligencer* in town," the man warned. "If he hears that you've—"

"He won't," the Kid interrupted. "'Cause we're going someplace where they'll not hear screams and a dead man can't tell lying stories later."

At noon Dusty entered the office and found three of his deputies waiting.

"I had to kill that Otley feller, Dusty," Waco began. "But Lon and Doc got their pair alive."

"And talking," the Kid went on.

"I never figured we'd get all three," Dusty said. "And Otley's the one I reckoned'd cause us most fuss. Mark still out?"

"Going the rounds, muttering what he's fixing to do to you given a real good chance," grinned Waco. "With that soft-shell on his tracks like a dog-hound hunting a bitch in heat."

"Did the trail crews agree to help, Dusty?" Doc inquired.

"All of 'em," Dusty replied.

Wanting to avoid any chance of incidents, Dusty had taken steps to avoid them. After seeing his deputies off to their various tasks, he had collected his paint stallion and ridden out to the trail crews' camps. There he interviewed the trail bosses and explained the situation. Refusing novel suggestions for removing Proudman, he secured a promise that each crew would be on its best behavior until the reporter departed. Relieved of one problem, Dusty returned to find his plans working well.

"Those two jaspers we laid hold of, Dusty," the Kid said. "They talked up a storm, but they won't be saying any more."

"How come?"

"After they'd telled us everything they knew, me 'n' Doc told *them* what'd happen should they start complaining about how they come to be so all-fired helpful."

"Are they marked up any?" Dusty asked.

"Naw!" snorted the Kid indignantly. "Like Miss Boyd done told us, the hardest part of getting folks to talk's starting 'em thinking what'll happen if they shouldn't."

A faint grin twisted Dusty's face. Miss Belle Boyd,* the legendary Rebel Spy, could claim to be an expert in the art of making reluctant people talk. If the Kid and Doc had applied her methods, their victims would carry no signs of ill-treatment, or be no worse than badly frightened.

"From what they say, Coulton put them up to it," Doc told Dusty. "They'd got to grab off Mrs. O'Hagen and the gal while Otley made sure Raz did what they wanted: tell that soft-shell he'd asked Mark and me to end the fight last night but we wouldn't unless he paid us. Then if Raz ever decided to change his story, them, or somebody like them'd get to his family again."

"Coulton must be *loco* to reckon that'd have us run out of town," Waco said.

"Not if he could get enough other stories like it in the *Intelligencer,*" Dusty corrected. "The Governor'd be forced to remove us from office, or likely get pushed out of his own. And we wouldn't be any too pleased with Raz when the story came out. Likely Coulton hoped there'd be fuss between us and him."

"What're we going to do, Dusty?" asked the Kid.

"Go and arrest Mr. Coulton," the small Texan replied. "I sure hope that Mark keeps that damned soft-shell out of the way until it's over."

Despite knowing how important a part he was playing, Mark felt bored with Dusty's plan. Whenever he went in the town during the morning, Proudman followed on his trail. Knowing that Dusty must be left free from the reporter's interference, Mark kept well clear of the Golden Nugget, O'Hagen's home and the school. Shortly after noon,

*Belle Boyd's story is in *The Colt and the Saber, The Rebel Spy, The Bad Bunch.*

Mark returned to the hotel. Without realizing that the big Texan roomed at the hotel, Proudman followed him into the dining room. Mouth-watering aromas wafted out from the kitchen. Forgetting to check the contents of his wallet, Proudman ordered a meal. As he ate, he wondered if the editor would refund the expenses for a trip that offered such barren results.

After expending considerable time and effort, the reporter found himself with little to show. Such businessmen as he had questioned admitted, some a touch grudgingly, to an improvement in conditions since the Texans took over. Figuring the trail crews would stand by their kind, so producing nothing he might use, he asked them no questions. Much to his disappointment, an assortment of gandy-dancers and buffalo hunters asserted profanely that at last they were receiving a fair deal in the town. Alert for the possibility, Mayor Galt left on urgent business before he could be interviewed and forced into a direct comment by Proudman. In his desperation to find something on which he might spin a damning tissue of half-truths to ruin the hated Texans, the reporter lavished drinks on a variety of trail-town idlers and loafers. While they might have furnished him with "genuine" stories of peace officer atrocities, the arrival of Mark and Doc, making the rounds, caused a marked desire to be elsewhere. So Proudman found he had expended all his cash for nothing. Figuring that Coulton would be generous, he gave the lack of funds no thought and did not realize he carried nothing with which to pay for the meal.

A well-dressed woman passed along the sidewalk and glanced through the window. Soon after she entered the dining room and went straight to Mark's table.

"Mr. Counter," she said. "Can you help me?"

"I'll try, ma'am," Mark promised, knowing the words carried to the reporter. "What's wrong?"

"It's my little boy, Jimmy. He's been seeing a lot of a roughneck who hangs around town. I heard him telling one of his friends that he and this Clegg were planning to hold up Po—Mr. Ericks' store. Of course I thought it was only a joke. But Jimmy took his father's two horses and the Ballard."

"Has he done that before, ma'am?" Mark asked, already on his feet from Mrs. Griddle's arrival.

"No. Of course George taught him to saddle the horses and use the rifle. But he's never offered to take either without asking for permission. And there's a lot of food gone from the kitchen."

"I'll see about it, ma'am," Mark promised.

Even as he headed for the door, Mark saw Proudman rise. If Clegg should be planning to rob the store, no time must be wasted in stopping him. Yet Mark did not want to be hampered by the reporter trailing along. Not that the blond giant hesitated. A boy's future depended on his being prevented from taking part in the robbery. With that at stake, Mark did not care what the *Intelligencer* printed about his handling of the situation.

Shoving back his chair, Proudman started to follow Mark out. The waiter saw the reporter rise and let out a yell. So intent on grabbing a chance of a story was Proudman that he had forgotten something of importance. Before he reached the door of the dining room, a big shape loomed in his path. Halting, he looked at the cold face of the hotel's manager.

"Going some place, friend?" the man asked.

"And in a hurry," Proudman answered, used to more respect from the lower classes.

"In such a hurry that you forgot to pay for the meal?"

"Oh! Is that all?" Proudman demanded, reaching into his jacket to withdraw then open the wallet. "I'll—I— Look, I don't have any money with me—"

"Now fancy that," said the manager in mock surprise.

"I bet the fairies done snuck it away from him while he ate all that good food," the waiter went on.

"Damn it, I'm a reporter for the *Kansas City Intelligencer*," Proudman squawked, always a way of avoiding trouble in the town of his origin. No hotel owner in Kansas City would dare to address him with disrespect, or object to his walking out without paying for a meal. Unfortunately Trail End was not Kansas City.

"Sure," agreed the manager. "And the last one was the chairman of the railroad's son. Into the kitchen."

"Why—?"

"Them as eats here pays for it—or works for it," the manager explained, holding a useful fist under the reporter's nose. "I've had a lousy day one way and another. Don't fuss me none or you're plumb likely to wish you hadn't."

Shorn of his paper's protection, Proudman lacked the courage to raise any objections. Swearing under his breath that he would make the manager pay for such treatment, he allowed himself to be escorted into the kitchen and put to work.

Already beginning to raise misgivings, Jimmy stood in the store and learned that being an outlaw possessed none of the excitement and glamour he expected. Much to his surprise, the short, grey-haired old owner showed no inclination to meekly obey orders. Not that Pop Ericks was foolish enough to offer active resistance to an armed, masked man when the cash drawer held only a few dollars.

"Where's the rest?" Clegg demanded.

"In the bank," Ericks replied.

Lashing around his empty left hand, Clegg slapped the old man across the mouth. As Ericks spun around and hit the counter, Jimmy let out a yell.

"Don't you hurt him, Darby Clegg!"

Swinging around, Clegg sent the youngster staggering as he lunged forward. Fury gripped the bearded man. In his protest Jimmy had given away a vital piece of information. That meant Clegg could not leave either Jimmy or Ericks alive when he pulled out. With those two horses used as a relay team, he ought to be able to outrun even the Kid's white stallion.

Feet thudded on the sidewalk and the door burst open. Coming through, Mark held a Colt in his right hand and recognized Clegg despite the mask.

"Drop it, or use it, hard man!" the blond giant challenged.

Hurriedly Clegg flung his gun aside. "Don't shoot, deputy!" he yelled.

Sitting on the floor with his bandana mask hanging around his neck, Jimmy stared first at the man he had thought to be so tough, then to the big Texan.

"All right, hard man," Mark said, twirling his Colt away. "Let's see just how tough you are."

Letting out a bellow more than half fear, Clegg charged across the room at the big deputy. Such tactics might work fine against his usual run of opponents, but failed miserably when tried on a man of Mark's fistic ability. Out drove Mark's big right fist, halting the charge. Then the left whipped across to the side of the other's jaw and the right sent Clegg sprawling to the floor.

"Whup him good, deputy!" Ericks whooped. "To hell with it if you bust a few things. Teach him respect for a feeble oldster like me."

Even without the permission Mark aimed to do just that. Given the storekeeper's wholehearted approbation, he went to work with a will. Coward Clegg might be, but he fought back with a rat-like courage and knew some about dirty brawling. However in any style of fighting, from refined to filthy, he rated yearling stock against Mark's professorial skill.

Coldly, savagely, mercilessly Mark handed Clegg the thrashing of his life. Nor did memory of injured dignity that morning account for the severity of his treatment. That youngster who sat staring open-mouthed had almost become a criminal through Clegg, and he had a perverted idea of what a tough man should be. Mark wanted to make certain that Jimmy never again regarded outlaws, or cheap hard-cases, as being men to look on as heroic.

Attracted by thuds and crashes, a small crowd gathered

outside the store. Mark took his eyes off a whining, mercy-begging Clegg and growled to Ericks:

"Get the kid out of here!"

"Sure," the old timer answered, taking Jimmy's ear between a powerful finger and thumb. Leading the youngster to the side door, he let him out and applied the toe of his boot in the appropriate place. "Get on home, blast ye!"

Scooping Clegg up from the floor, Mark slammed him against the wall. Ignoring moans from the man not to be hit any more, he gave a warning.

"You mention that button's part in your game and I'll make this look like starters. Now get the hell out of here."

"Danged fool kid," Ericks grunted. "Still, it could've gone worse for him."

"You've never been righter," Mark agreed and looked around, wondering where Proudman might be. "Sending in his story, likely," he mused. "Well, the hell with him and the *Intelligencer*. That kid's future's more important than what might happen to me."

Such was the floating outfit's reputation in Trail End that they arrested Coulton without intervention by his men. When he tried to draw his gun, Dusty pistol-whipped him to the ground and hauled him to the jail. On his recovery, Coulton overheard a conversation specially prepared for his benefit.

"Well, that's the last of 'em, Lon," Dusty was saying from the passage outside the cell. "We've cleaned out Trail End."

"Yep," agreed the Kid. "Funny though, I allus thought Eggars'd be one we'd get trouble from. But he's straight and's been real helpful."

"Sure has. Say, I hope that he manages to raise the money he needs to buy the theater and those three saloons."

"And me. With him running 'em, there'll be no more trouble."

"What's that you say?" Coulton demanded, rising and lurching to the door of the cell.

"Oh, you're awake are you," Dusty grunted in well-simulated surprise. "I was just saying how I hope Eggars can raise the money for your place."

"Eggars!" Coulton spat out.

"Sure. If we can get an honest man running the theater, Good Fortune, First Chance and Blazing Pine, our work's done."

At another time Coulton might have sensed a trap. Still dazed from the blow to his jaw with the barrel of Dusty's left hand Colt, filled with thoughts of how he might avoid standing trial on a charge of attempted kidnapping, he reacted as the small Texan hoped.

"Honest!" he squawked, grabbing the bars and shaking them. "Why it was him who egged the rest of us on."

"G'wan!" sniffed the Kid. "You're just saying that out of ornery meanness."

"Oh yeah! Well it was Eggars who gave Jackley the scatter and sent him after you, Fog. Hones—"

"Where's the marshal?" shouted a voice from the office. "I demand to see the marshal."

Instantly Coulton's mouth snapped shut. Fighting down the annoyance he felt, for he knew the man would not continue speaking, Dusty turned and walked from the cell [illegible]. In the office he found an indignant-faced Proudman confronting the other members of the floating outfit.

"Look here, marshal!" Proudman began, waving hands reddened by a long period of dish-washing at the hotel. "I've heard a disturbing report that one of your deputies brutally beat a man he was arresting."

"You saw him do it?" Dusty asked.

"No, but—"

"You've a witness who saw him?"

"Ye— Well, not exactly—"

"Then you've no real proof—" Dusty began.

"To hell with it, Dusty!" Mark put in and faced the reporter. "Yeah, I did hand a licking to a feller. And I'd do it again."

"The *Intelligencer*'s readers will be interested to hear how their Governor's appointees handle the law," Proudman stated, taking out his notebook.

"Just you listen to me, you stinking soft-shell!" Mark growled, looming before the man. "Because of you being on my heels this morning, I couldn't stop that yahoo mean-mouthing me in the street. So a kid got the idea he was a man to be respected. You get fool ideas like that when you're young—"

"Only most kids grow out of them when they're older," Doc put in.

"Some do, some don't," Mark continued. "This one would've seen Clegg for what he was, had I been able to handle him right. Only I couldn't, because if you had seen me, you'd have printed a load of lies about me in your newspaper. So Jimmy Griddle looked up to Clegg enough to try to help him rob the store. I stopped him just in time. Go print what the hell you like. I'd do the same again."

At that moment Grosvenor arrived with a demand to see his client. Realizing how close to breaking point Mark's temper was, Dusty told him to go with the lawyer. Proudman watched with growing concern as Dusty and Mark left. Then he backed to the wall, all his superior condescension falling from him, as the remaining trio moved in his direction.

"Your sort turn my guts," Doc told him in cold contempt. "You're so rotten with envy when you see somebody who's got something you haven't, or can do something you can't, that all you can think of's bringing him down to your stinking level. Why'd you think Coulton had you sent here?"

"So that I could report on the way you Texans ran the law."

"You mean how we compared with that fine figure of honest law-upholding who held the badge afore we come?" Doc inquired.

"Y-yes—"

"The hell that's why he sent for you!" Waco spat out. "Coulton brought you in knowing you'd jump for any chance to spread filthy lies about us. That'd make folks ask the Governor to bust us out of here, or lose his office. Then Coulton's kind could bring in another murdering skunk like Jackley to wear the badge. *That's* why he brought you in, *hombre*."

At the back of his heart, especially after what he had learned since arriving, Proudman knew the youngster spoke the truth. Yet his intellectual bigotry and hatred of anybody who dared oppose his views refused to let him admit it.

"You know that fight last night?" asked Doc. "The one you reckon we ought to have bust heads to stop— And if we'd gone in sooner, that'd been the only way to stop it."

"There's only your word for that," Proudman whined.

"You heard Raz O'Hagen, the owner, say we acted right," Doc reminded him. "Only you aimed to see him again, when we weren't there, to scare him into talking your way. Well, mister, you'd've found he changed his mind."

"Not because he wanted to though," drawled the Kid. "But because Coulton hired fellers to see Raz, grab off his wife and daughter and use them to make him tell the lies you wanted to hear."

"I-I know nothing of that!" Proudman gulped. "All I know is that big deputy beat a man needlessly—"

"And that's what you'll print," Waco said.

"The *Intelligencer*—"

"Prints what it sees or hears some times but not others," Doc interrupted. "Even if doing it could run the straightest Governor this State's ever had out of office. Coulton sure knew what he was doing, sending for you."

"I mind when we ran the law back in Quiet Town," the Kid remarked in a conversational tone. "There was a stinking soft-shell newspaperman just like you all set to print lies about us. Only he had him some bad luck."

"How— How do you mean?" Proudman gulped.

"Got word of a story one night and went to look into it. Only on the way he walked into a wild hoss that near on kicked him to pieces. We never could figure out how that there hoss come to be in town."

"Feller's troubles didn't end there even," Doc carried on when the Kid stopped. "Seemed like the regular doctor was out of town so they asked a cowhand like me who knowed a mite about doctoring to see to him. This cowhand made a mistake in the dark. He knew the feller had a bad busted leg that'd have to come off and did a real neat job—only he got the wrong leg, first crack."

"Are you threat—" Proudman began.

"Doctor went out of town this morning, didn't he, Lon?" Waco asked mildly.

"And won't be back until tomorrow," the Kid agreed. "Say, I hope I remembered to fasten that mean ole hoss of mine up good. If he got out and somebody walked in on him—by accident— Waal, he wouldn't be too happy about it at-all."

For the first time in his life Proudman knew real fear. Suddenly he realized the trio's motives. They were threatening him in that veiled manner to save their friend from future trouble. It had been his intention to demand Mark's arrest on a charge of assault and, guessing that, the other three had come to the big Texan's aid. While Proudman doubted if the incident had happened in Quiet Town, he felt sure that it would if one word of complaint appeared in the *Intelligencer*. Nothing about the grim-visaged young men before him hinted that they might only be bluffing. Nor would the fact that he wrote the story in Kansas City save him from their vengeance. Men who guided a trail herd across the trackless miles from Texas to the railroad markets would experience little difficulty in going from Trail End to Kansas City. Gifted with imagination, he could almost see himself attacked by a savage horse as he went about town. The thought terrified him.

"Wha— What do you want me to do?" he whined.

"Nothing at all, except get the hell out of our sight," Doc replied. "And that as soon as you can make it. There's an eastbound train leaving any time now."

Turning, the reporter slunk from the office. Soon after Mark and Dusty came from the cell area at the rear of the building, following Grosvenor who spoke over his shoulder.

"So you intend to hold my client?"

"Unless you can produce legal authority otherwise," Dusty agreed, secure in the knowledge that the local Justice of the Peace had left town to avoid such authority being obtained.

"On the unsupported testimony of those two men?"

"No, counselor. For attempted murder. He tried to pull a gun on me. It's in the desk drawer there."

"Very well," Grosvenor breathed. "I wish to lodge a formal complaint—"

"That's your rightful privilege," Dusty assured him. "All right, you bunch. Let's have you earning your pay."

Grosvenor looked around the office, hoping to see Proudman. Failing, he left and hurried to his premises in search of his clerk. Although the clerk went around town, he failed to locate Proudman. Without even returning to his hotel, the reporter caught the train and counted himself lucky to be able to do so.

"Where's that lousy soft-shell?" Mark demanded, glaring around.

"Got tired of waiting and left," replied the Kid in a tone which told Dusty and Mark he considered the matter closed.

"What happened back there?" Waco inquired.

"Coulton's not going to tell us any more," Dusty answered, aware that asking about the reporter's departure would be futile. "He won't even confirm what he told us about Eggars."

"Damn all law-wranglers!" Waco groaned. "They should—"

"Not all lawyers, boy," Dusty interrupted. "Just Grosvenor's kind."

"We could maybe get Coulton to change his mind," the Kid suggested.

"Not by tricking him any more, and that's all I'd let you try," Dusty answered. "Damn it, though. I hoped we could fix Eggars. Then we can think about heading for home."

"We could maybe run him out if we caught him using crooked gambling gear," Doc remarked. "You know, under that gambling ordinance you had Galt bring in, Dusty."

"He'd never do it," Mark objected. "He's too smart for that."

"I don't know," Doc commented, extending an apparently empty hand above the desk and giving it a shake. Two nickels bounced on to the desk's top. "He just might at that."

PART SIX

Eggars' Try

Standing on the platform of a day coach in the east-bound train, Eggars scowled his hate at the half-circle of watchful Texans.

"You'll not get away with this, Fog," he warned. "Those cards and dice were planted on me."

"Prove it and I'll toss whoever did it in the pokey," Dusty answered. "All I *know* is that we found four decks of 'readers' and a fair slew of loaded dice in your place. So I've closed you and I'm running you out of town."

In a way Eggars could claim a fair reason for complaining. The cards found on the blackjack tables and dice taken from the hooligan or high-dice layouts were certainly all Dusty said and came from Eggars' saloon; but they had been in the safe at the marshal's office since Doc's first inspection. Skilled sleight-of-hand on the part of Doc, then Waco, saw the items returned under the noses of an interested crowd. Presented with the "evidence", Dusty acted as he would if it had been real, by closing the saloon and ordering its owner from town. Once again the reputation of the floating outfit, backed by the menace of the customers who believed they had been cheated, prevented trouble. By the middle of the afternoon, Eggars and the bulk of his staff found themselves on a train headed east.

Dishonest? Possibly. Immoral? Maybe. But the items originated from Eggars' saloon and had been used to cheat players in the games. Like the other owners, Eggars had failed to anticipate Doc's knowledge and retained cards and dice he felt could not be detected as dishonest, using Jordan's excuse for their presence when caught. Also the saloonkeeper had sent Jackley on the murder mission that ended in the ex-marshal's death. So Dusty felt that the end justified the means. While Eggars had run his place honestly since the inspection and confiscation of the crooked gambling gear, Dusty knew he would return to his old practices as soon as the floating outfit started for home and a more permanent marshal took over.

Word of the latest closure passed around the town and a number of people, far in excess of the normal train-departure watchers, gathered to see what happened. Glaring around, Eggars tried to gauge the feeling of the onlookers to his eviction. He thought sufficient of them showed concern for him to give a warning.

"I'll be back!" he snarled, eyes raking the crowd and fixing momentarily on any face which showed a sign of wavering. "You just bet that I'll be back. And when I come, there'll be no sitting on the fence. Them who aren't for me'll be on the other side."

The train's whistle shrilled out before Dusty could answer the threat. Then it began to move slowly away from the depot, with Eggars standing grim-faced and menacing on the platform looking back.

Dusty watched the train's departure with mixed feelings. Although he felt some satisfaction at disposing of the last, and probably most dangerous, of the town's crooked element, he wondered if the affair would end so tamely. If

Eggars did not return, the floating outfit's work in Trail End was over. Provided the town wanted it that way, any reasonably efficient peace officer could hold it under control and prevent a return to the bad days so recently ended.

Behind the small Texan, a discussion rumbled among the assembled citizens. It seemed that Eggars' implied threat had struck home hard and aroused a fair amount of concern.

"Eggars won't let it go that easy," Elsom, the undertaker announced loudly. "He'll be coming back and he won't come alone."

"If he does come back," Dinger Magee growled, coming from the yard-master's office and surveying the crowd with disfavor, "you'll likely get some trade, Mr. Elsom."

"Yeah," agreed the undertaker. "Only who'll I be laying away?"

"It could be some of us," muttered another man gloomily.

"Eggars had some tough cusses working for him," a third in the crowd continued, darting worried glances around.

"And they sang real low when Cap'n Fog went by 'em," Magee answered. "Come on, some of you. If you ain't got work to do, me 'n' my lumpers have."

Slowly the crowd began to disintegrate, its dispersal increasing as various members found themselves being left by the others. As if wanting to avoid any chance of being asked to take sides, men scuttled away hurriedly.

"You reckon Eggars'll be back, Dusty?" Waco asked, eyeing the hurried departures with sardonic gaze.

"I don't know, boy," Dusty admitted.

"One thing's for certain sure," drawled the Kid. "Happen he does come back, it'll be with enough help to make things real interesting."

"And like he said," drawled Mark. "When he comes, there'll be no sitting on the fence. Anybody who doesn't side him, should he win out, won't last a week here in town."

"Thing I want to know's where's that lard-gutted law-wrangler," the Kid commented. "I'd've thought he'd be round here defending another client."

"Maybe we've plumb discouraged him," grinned Waco.

"And maybe we've not," Dusty answered. "Wherever he is, you can bet he's cooking up something to help Eggars."

Which proved to be a mighty shrewd guess on Dusty's part. Having heard of Eggars' eviction, Grosvenor had set about putting into operation a plan concocted for such an eventuality. Visiting a local businessman, the lawyer made certain demands and the other was in no position to refuse. After making full arrangements, Grosvenor uttered several threats if there should be any mishaps and left the man to his work.

Calling at the jail to see Coulton, the lawyer silenced his client's complaints with an assurance that all would be well.

"It'd better be," the saloonkeeper warned. "Because if Eggars doesn't get me out, I'll tell Fog everything I know."

"Don't worry," Grosvenor hissed, darting a glance to where Waco was leaning against the wall at the other end of the passage. "Everything's fixed up. Eggars will take care of you when he comes back."

"It'd better not be too long before he comes," Coulton warned. "I'm a real impatient man."

"I said don't worry. It won't be long," Grosvenor answered and raised his voice. "I'm through, deputy. You can let me out."

While Marshal James Butler Hickok of Abilene could only be termed an active peace officer at certain times, he felt the gathering of professional men at Saloon Sixteen called for investigation. Two or three members of the hired gun profession might come together without arousing more than casual interest; but when at least twenty paid fighting men met, Hickok took notice. Hickok took as few chances as possible, a fact that had already cost a deputy and friend his life when he incautiously came up behind the marshal in a gun fight.

Having received a telegraph message from Dusty Fog warning of Eggars' eviction from Trail End, Hickok had made a point of meeting the east-bound train. He saw the saloonkeeper leave it and tailed him to Saloon Sixteen.

Six foot three in height, with a giant's frame clad in stylish, expensive gambler's fashion, yellow hair hanging shoulder-long from beneath his broad-brimmed Stetson, "Wild Bill" Hickok looked every inch the man highly colored stories in the *Police Gazette* and other such magazines portrayed. A man of direct action, he took steps to learn what brought the meeting about.

After some talk from Eggars, which Hickok—standing on the sidewalk and watching through the window—could not hear, one of the men left the table. From the direction he took, Hickok guessed he was going to answer the call of nature. With an encyclopedic knowledge of the town's geography, the marshal knew where to find the man.

Coming out of the backhouse, his wants satisfied, the man felt a hand clamp on his shoulder. Before he could draw his gun, he crashed into the building with enough force to wind him. Nor did he feel inclined to complete the draw on discovering his assailant was Wild Bill Hickok.

"What's it all about, bucko?" demanded the marshal, thrusting a cocked Colt Cavalry Peacemaker unde the man's chin.

"Eggars's hiring guns to take back to Trail End," the man answered. "He's fixing to run Dusty Fog's bunch out of town."

"Would he be getting many takers?"

"Every one of us. He allows the folks in town'll either stay out of it, or come in on our side."

"Forget the 'our' bit," Hickok said. "You're going to jail until after I've let Dusty know what's headed his way."

"That being the case," the man answered. "You don't need to turn me loose until after the others've gone."

No great desire to see law and order triumph caused Hickok's actions. The time might come when he needed help from a man of Dusty Fog's proven ability and the Rio Hondo gun wizard never forgot a good turn. So Hickok obligingly jailed the man on a charge of being drunk, then went to the Abilene telegraph office and sent a message over the wires to Trail End.

WARNING

I am coming back to Trail End with fifty men. If Dusty Fog and his deputies are there when I arrive, the citizens of Trail End will regret it.

Overnight posters bearing the threatening words appeared in prominent places around Trail End and attracted much attention. People gathered around each of the posters, ignoring the fact that all showed signs of having been produced in a hurry, reading the words. While the message carried no signature, every person who saw it knew that Eggars was the "I" mentioned.

One of the earliest students of the posters had been Mayor Galt. Roused from his bed by an excited servant, he dressed hurriedly, took in the sight and headed for the marshal's office. He found Dusty seated at the desk holding a telegraph message form.

"Those signs all over town—!" Galt began.

"I've seen 'em," Dusty answered.

"Eggars's bluffing—isn't he?"

"I'd be real surprised if he is, mayor," Dusty said, holding out the piece of paper. "Read this."

"Bu-but this reached you last night!" the mayor squawked, after reading the message. "Hickok told you they're coming."

"Sure."

"Why didn't you let me know?"

"Shucks, there wasn't any great hurry," Dusty answered. "And I didn't want folks getting all worried without good cause."

"Wha-what do you intend to do?"

"What Governor Mansfield brought me here to do," Dusty answered. "What did you reckon I'd do, mayor, run?"

A disgruntled and perturbed man left Dusty's office. Down by the railroad depot a crowd had gathered and Galt made his way towards them. Practically every man in town formed the group and their eyes turned to Galt as he walked along the street in their direction.

"We've got to send them Texans out of town," Elsom announced. "Hey. Here's Mayor Galt, been to see Fog. Let's ask him what's doing."

Alert as always for signs of public opinion, Galt scanned the faces before him and tried to gauge the feelings behind them. He read worry, fear, uncertainty on some faces; but there were others in the crowd who showed no such emotions. Enough for Galt to hesitate in making a direct statement.

"I've seen Captain Fog," he said. "He already knew about this message."

"What'd he say?" demanded Elsom.

"That he aims to stay here," the mayor replied.

"He can't do that!" yelled a querulous voice.

"Damn it, Galt," Elsom went on. "You're the mayor. Tell Fog to take his pards and get the hell out of town."

"What's up, Elsom?" Dinger Magee growled, stepping out before the crowd to face the undertaker. "Has your business gone down since Cap'n Fog took over?"

"What's that mean?" Elsom spat.

Ignoring the man, Magee swung towards the crowd. Cold contempt glinted in his eyes as he studied the frightened members of it. Ever since the Texans arrived, the railroad yard-master had backed them in every way he could. It had been Magee who gave the warning when he saw Jackley waiting to ambush Dusty on the first night. Nothing in the small Texan's subsequent behavior caused him to regret the chance he had taken. At last it seemed that Trail End stood a chance of becoming cleansed of the men who had made the town's reputation for evil and corruption. For the first time Dusty and the floating outfit needed help. Dinger Magee was going to do his damnedest to see that they received it.

"You bunch turn my guts," he said. "Look at Trail End now and think back to what it was like afore those Texas boys came here. They've risked their lives, for damned little money, to make Trail End fit to live. Now because some lousy thief threatens to come here with a few men, you're wanting them to be run out."

"There'll be fifty of 'em!" Elsom pointed out.

"If he's got that many," Magee countered. "And I can see at least seventy grown men here in front of me. Not counting the trail crews who'll be backing Cap'n Fog, and the railroad men."

"You can count the buffler-hunters in on this here election, Dinger," called a member of that trade who stood at the rear. "I know who I'd rather see running the town—and it ain't a nose-wiping dude saloonkeeper neither."

Silence fell as the listening men digested the words. Only a few of them were directly involved in operating saloons and none failed to recognize what the town had become before the Texans' arrival. Slowly talk welled up again until it rolled out in deep-throated volume.

"Let's go see Cap'n Fog!" somebody yelled and others took up the cry.

"Well," Elsom said to Galt, watching the crowd move off in the direction of the marshal's office. "What're you going to do?"

"The same as I always do," replied the mayor. "Go along with the majority."

And, saying that, he followed the citizens whose votes could keep him in office.

"Meeting along the street, Dusty," the Kid remarked, looking through the window. "Looks like them posters done got folks all stirred up."

"There'll be some who want us to run, likely," Mark guessed.

"What'll you do if they ask you to, Dusty?" Doc asked.

"What'd you do?" Dusty countered.

"There's some'd say we don't owe the folks here a thin dime or drop of good Texas blood," Doc replied.

"How about that feller who warned Dusty when Jackley laid for him?" Waco demanded hotly. "Whoever he is, he rates higher than having us run out."

"All I said was there's some who'd say it," Doc answered with a grin. "I'm for doing what we come here to do."

"Here they come," announced the Kid.

"We'll soon know which way they stand," Mark went on.

Feet thudded on the street, then the sound died away as the citizens formed up before the office.

"We want Cap'n Fog!" yelled a voice.

"Come on out here, Cap'n Fog!" shouted another.

Crossing the room, Dusty opened the door and stepped outside. Instantly the slight movement ended and a complete silence fell on the crowd. Dinger Magee broke it, advancing from the mass and looking up at the small Texan whose life he had saved.

"You've seen these here posters, Cap'n Fog," he said.

"I've seen 'em."

"What we want to know is how you stand on what they say."

"In other words," Titmuss went on after Magee finished, "are you staying on here to meet Eggars and his hired guns?"

"We're sticking," Dusty told the crowd. "Let Eggars make this play and Trail End's his town. He'll suck you dry and spit you out when he's done. Governor Mansfield brought me in to clean Eggars' kind out of town. That being the case, I'm staying on here until I've done it."

Nobody made any reply for a time. Looking around, Dusty waited to hear if the work the floating outfit had done, the risks they had taken, were justified. At such a time, a lawman learned if he rated the respect of the ordinary folks who helped pay his salary.

"You're set on it, Cap'n?" Magee asked.

"We're set!" Dusty stated.

"Then there's only one thing us folks here can do," the yard-master declared and stepped forward with his hand held out to Dusty. "Put ourselves up as your deputies. Tell us what you want doing and we'll see it's done."

"Good for you, Cap'n Fog!" yelled O'Hagen, moving up to Magee's side.

Never a man to miss a chance, Mayor Galt passed around the side of the crowd and moved to Dusty's side. Raising his hands, he waved the people to silence.

"It's the bounden duty of every Trail End citizen to give Captain Fog his support!" he announced. "Now it's not my intention to make a speech—"

"That's fine, mayor, because we don't have time to listen to one," O'Hagen shouted and a roar of laughter greeted the comment.

"As our good friend states, we don't," Galt agreed, grinning in his best professional vote-grabbing manner. "So let's hear what you want us to do, Cap'n Fog and, by cracky, we'll do it."

Riding at the head of some twenty hard-cases, Eggars' floor manager nodded towards where the trail they used became the town's main street, indicating the three figures standing across it.

"Looks like they've got a welcome committee waiting," he said. "What the hell's that lard-gutted mayor doing with Leroy and the Kid?"

"Maybe that feller sent the wrong word about how folks in town feel," one of the men remarked.

"Grosvenor wouldn't dare cross the boss!" the floor manager growled.

Yet it had happened. Always trying to think ahead of the opposition, Dusty had guessed that Eggars would want to know how the citizens were taking his warning. So the small Texan sent the Kid and Waco to the telegraph office before going out to face the crowd. When Grosvenor arrived to pass a warning of the citizens' reaction, the two deputies prevented him from doing so. Ignoring the lawyer's protests, they hustled him off to jail on the flimsy excuse that he was disturbing the peace. Nor did his clerk have any greater success later, being informed by the telegraph operator that the line was down. When he tried to hire a horse, the livery barn owner refused and an attempt to take one led to his arrest. So Eggars failed to learn of the true state of affairs. Satisfied that the citizens would not back Dusty Fog, the saloonkeeper went forward with his plans.

"That's close enough," warned the Kid, rifle cradled across his arm.

"You figure to stop us going in?" asked the floor manager.

"We're fixing to do just that," agreed the Kid.

"Just the two of you?" Eggars' man grinned. "Or do you reckon having Galt along makes a difference."

"I'm here in my official capacity, Keets," Galt boomed. "And I'm warning you that Trail End doesn't want your kind."

"You're been under the sun without a hat if you reckon those two beef-heads can stop us, Galt."

"And you should learn to count if you reckon there'll only be the two of us stopping you," Doc commented. "Come ahead—but afore you do it, look along the street there."

At the same moment the Kid let out a shrill whistle. Instantly armed men appeared from the ends of buildings, at windows, on the roofs. Nor did the threat end there. To the left of the trail more men came into sight: Texas trail crews, guns displayed prominently.

"Up the other side there're maybe a dozen hide-hunters lining buffalo guns at you," the Kid said.

"Eggars allowed there'd be no trouble from the locals," one of the hard-cases announced in a worried voice.

"If you reckon that," drawled the Kid. "Come ahead."

For a moment none of the men spoke, and all controlled their horses' movements. Paid fighting men, they could balance the odds and knew the opposition held all the cards. One of the men behind Keets expressed aloud what the others thought.

"Going in there'd be riding into a death-trap."

"I was paid to fight, not commit suicide," another declared.

"You do what you want to do, Keets," announced a third. "But I'm getting the hell out of here."

Which sentiment received almost complete approval. Keets gave a shrug and made as if to leave. Starting to turn his horse away to the right, he grabbed for his gun with the hidden hand. Too late he found that the move had not fooled either Doc or the Kid. Even as Keets drew the Colt and slanted it across his body, Doc's revolver flashed from leather. Not quite as fast, the Kid brought the rifle from his arm, its flat bark echoing the deeper crack of Doc's Colt. Both bullets tore into Keets' body before he could fire a shot and he tumbled lifeless from his saddle.

Realizing the danger, the hard-cases swung their horses wildly around. At any moment lead might start pouring down the slopes from the buffalo rifles, or lashing at them out of the trail crews' weapons.

"Don't shoot 'em!" Doc roared, knowing the danger as well as did the hired gun-hands.

The order was relayed by the watching trail bosses to their men and the hard-cases fled without another shot being fired. On the other side of town, the west-bound train drew to a halt at the depot.

"The town's mighty quiet, boss," said the gun-hung tough who followed Eggars from the train.

"I told the others to time their ride in with the train arriving," the saloonkeeper answered, darting glances around and noting the deserted aspect.

Not that the lack of people surprised him. If Grosvenor

had played his part correctly, the posters should have given warning of Eggars' coming. So the good citizens of Trail End, having been allowed a day to think of the consequences, would be staying under cover. The fact that Grosvenor had sent no word to the contrary led Eggars to assume that the people of the town were acting as he expected they would.

Even Grosvenor's absence failed to surprise Eggars. Despite his other excellent qualities, the lawyer displayed a broad streak of caution and would be unlikely to chance coming into what might be a dangerous location.

Thinking of the lawyer's aversion to danger raised another point. Unless Eggars under-estimated Dusty Fog, the marshal and at least some of the deputies ought to be around. However, if Keets had played his part all should go as planned.

When making his arrangements, Eggars had decided Keets should circle the town and bring the men in from the west. That ought to take the floating outfit, expecting the attack to come from the east—if expecting an arrival by horseback at all—by surprise.

Various buildings hid the western side of town from the train passengers' view. So Eggars did not know his supporting party had failed to reach town and the train's noise drowned out the sound of the shots which had ended Keets' life.

"I don't like it," a second of Eggars' eight-man backing force muttered. "Things're too quiet—and we had the train to ourselves."

A warning passed down the track by Dinger Magee had ensured that there would be no innocent bystanders aboard the train to make the task of dealing with Eggars harder or more dangerous.

"Three of you stop on the platform and watch the other side," Eggars ordered, ignoring the comment. "The rest of you come with me."

Swinging down, the five men stood in a group behind

their employer. Then they stiffened, tensing like cougar watching a deer approach along a game trail. Dusty Fog, Mark Counter and Waco walked around the end of the yard-master's office. Although the small Texan had empty hands, the blond giant to his right and the tall youngster on his left each carried a shotgun in a position of readiness. Tall as the other two might be, at that moment Dusty Fog gave the impression of towering over them.

"Turn right round, Mr. Eggars," Dusty said.

Even before leaving the train, Eggars had taken the Gaulois squeezer-gun in its cigar-case disguise from his pocket. He wore a gunbelt, with a revolver in its holster, but had no intention of making use of the openly displayed weapon. Stepping away from his men, the saloonkeeper walked towards Dusty and put on a pleasant expression.

"Can't we talk this over, Captain Fog?" he inquired, raising his right hand as if meaning to open the cigar-case and offer its contents to the small Texan. His eyes measured the distance and his thumb rested on the firing stud ready to press. "If you'll listen to reason—"

Everything seemed to be going as Eggars wished, with the Texans completely fooled by his acting and the deadly hide-out squeeze-gun.

In that the saloonkeeper made the last and greatest mistake of his life. Ever since he killed the brothel-keeper with the Gaulois, Eggars had been under suspicion. Knowing that no .41 caliber bullet had struck Burger down, Dusty presented Doc with the unpleasant task of extracting the missile from the body. Although battered and misshapen by the impact, the piece of lead still served, by virtue of its weight, to confirm Dusty's suspicions.

With that fact established, Dusty gave thought to Eggars' motives for saying he used a Derringer. There could be only one possible answer. The saloonkeeper did not want the Texans to know the real type of weapon he used. Which meant he must carry a disguised gun of some description.

So Dusty went to face Eggars ready for some kind of

treachery. Alert for trouble, the small Texan studied the "cigar-case" and saw the hole through which the bullet would emerge.

Half a second later, an instant before Eggars pressed the Gaulois' trigger-stud, Dusty completed his conclusions and drew, to send a bullet into the saloonkeeper's head.

Then all hell burst loose.

Hands drove at guns as Eggars' men went into action. Two shotguns swiveled into line. At that range Mark and Waco did not need to raise their weapons beyond waist level. Already they had cocked the shotguns and needed only to squeeze the triggers. Four awesome bellows roared in a single rumble of sound and thirty-six buckshot balls ripped into Eggars' party. Flesh and blood could not face such a devastating volley. Two of the men slammed backwards, torn open by the lethal balls. All the other three on the ground felt lead gouge into them from the outer edges of the spreading pattern of the shot.

When drawing, Dusty had fetched out both guns. The left hand Colt wrote a finish to Eggar's career and a moment later flame lanced from the weapon in his right hand. One of the trio on the train reeled backwards, gun clattering from his fingers. Even as Mark and Waco dropped their empty shotguns, reaching for the waiting Colts, the last two of the invading force threw up their hands.

Men swarmed into sight, converging on the train which Dusty had insisted on meeting accompanied only by Mark and Waco.

"It's over, gents," Dusty told them. "Trail End's still your town."

"I'm sorry to see you go, Captain Fog," Mayor Galt said, shaking hands with the small Texan. "This town'll not seem the same without you."

"Let's hope it never gets to be the same, mayor," Dusty replied.

"You can be sure it won't," Erasmus O'Hagen stated,

standing with the rest of the party waiting to see the Texans depart. "We'll see to that."

Three days had passed since the death of Eggars. On his arrival from Texas, Shanghai Pierce declared himself well satisfied that justice had been done. A new marshal, young, keen, honest, came to replace Dusty; a man who could be relied on never to allow the town to return to its old ways.

So the floating outfit's work was done and they prepared to return to the Rio Hondo. Much the same crowd gathered as had stood around to watch their arrival, but the attitude of its members had changed. Now approval, mingled with a little sorrow, showed on every face as they watched the five young Texans riding in a loose V formation out of town.

"If anybody'd've asked me," Titmuss said, watching the Texans ride by, "I'd've sworn it couldn't be done."

"Yes, sir," Dinger Magee replied, raising his hand in a respectful salute to the leader of the floating outfit. "He's not tall and he don't talk loud, but Cap'n Fog's sure a town-taming man."